P9-DUH-524

THEY SHALL HAVE STARS

by the same author

*

CITIES IN FLIGHT

*

They Shall Have Stars

A SCIENCE FICTION NOVEL

by

JAMES BLISH

★

And death shall have no dominion
Dead men naked they shall be one
With the man in the wind and the west moon;
When their bones are picked clean and the
  clean bones gone,
They shall have stars at elbow and foot . . .

DYLAN THOMAS

FABER AND FABER LTD
3 Queen Square
London

First published in 1956
by Faber and Faber Limited
3 Queen Square, London WC1
Reprinted 1965, 1968 and 1974
Printed in Great Britain by
Whitstable Litho Straker Brothers Ltd.
All rights reserved

ISBN 0 571 06264 4

To
FREDERIK POHL

Author's Note

This first volume of *Cities in Flight* is a prologue to the work as a whole, and hence contains neither any flying cities nor any characters in common with the remaining three volumes. Instead, it undertakes to show the circumstances under which the two fundamental inventions which made the Okie cities possible were discovered—and the reasons why the cities found the nearer stars already scattered with colonists, ready to employ them, when the time for their own diaspora came round.

We begin in 2018 A.D.—imminent enough so that my "Premier Erdsenov" might be Brezhnev-Kosygin's successor—and the events here cover about two years. There is a leap of several centuries before *Cities in Flight* proper begins, and thereafter the action is continuous through the remaining three volumes, all the way to 4004 A.D. For what happened in the interim, and for a general skeleton of all the important events, the reader is referred to the overall Chronology at the end of this volume.

The writing of *Cities in Flight* occupied me, off and on, from 1948 to 1962, and like many such long projects, the order of composition of its parts wasn't orderly at all, and was further complicated by the publishing history (which is also appended). Briefly, however, the third volume, *Earthman, Come Home*, was written first, and was followed by the first volume—this one— to provide a "prequel." Then I wrote the ending, *A Clash of Cymbals*, and backtracked to the second volume, *A Life For The Stars*. Thus the novel as a whole contains some reminders of preceding events which economy would say it does not now need. But then, so does *The Ring of the Nibelung*, for similar reasons though to far nobler effect.

JAMES BLISH

New York
1964

CHRONOLOGY OF *Cities in Flight*

A.D.

2012 Bliss Wagoner elected Senator (D.) from Alaska. Dr. Guiseppi Corsi drummed out of the U.S. Bureau of Standards as a security risk.

2013 Joint Senate-House Committee on Space Flight launches the Jupiter Project. Department of Health, Education, Welfare and Security underwrites international conference on degenerative disease.

2015 Investigating subcommittee of the Senate Finance Committee votes to investigate the Bridge.

2016 Construction of the Proserpine Station begun.

2018 Bliss Wagoner re-elected. Discovery of ascomycin.

2019 Publication of the report on the Bridge investigation. Discovery of the Dillon–Wagoner graviton-polarity generator.

2020 Second investigation of the Bridge. Flight of Wagoner. The Believer Riots. The Orders of Extradition. Fall of the Bridge.

2021 Escape of the "Colonials" from the Jovian system. Trial and death of Wagoner. Death of Corsi, under questioning.

2022 The MacHinery–Erdsenov Agreement. The Cold Peace.

2027 Assassination of MacHinery. The Erdsenov Proclamation.

2032 Assassination of Erdsenov. The Terror. The Hamiltonian Exodus.

7

2039 Banning of space flight and all associated sciences on Earth, by the Krushchevgrad Proclamation.

2105 Fall of the West (an agreed arbitrary date).

2289 First colonial contact with the Vegan Tyranny.

2310 The Battle of Altair, first engagement of the Vegan War.

2375 Rediscovery of the spindizzy. Escape from Earth of the Thorium Trust's Plant No. 8.

2394 Height of the Earth Exodus. Rape of Thor V by the Interstellar Master Traders (*orig.* Gravitogorsk–Mars).

2413 Investment of Vega. Battle of the Forts. Scorching of the Vegan system by the Third Colonial Navy, under Adm. Hrunta.

2451 Alois Hrunta found guilty *in absentia* of atrocities and attempted genocide by the Colonial Court, Judge Schmitz presiding.

2464 Battle of BD 40°4048′. Alois Hrunta declares himself Emperor of Space.

2522 Collapse of the Bureaucratic State. The Police Interregnum. Proclamation of amnesty to the colonists. Beginning of the Empty Years.

2998 Birth of John Amalfi.

3089 Amalfi becomes mayor of Manhattan. Poisoning of Alois Hrunta. Balkanization of the Hruntan Empire.

3111 Manhattan leaves the Earth. Arpad Hrunta installed as Emperor of Space.

3200 Birth of Mark Hazleton. Anti-Earth pogrom in the Malar system; colonization of the Acolyte cluster.

3301 Manhattan violates its contract on Epoch; deFord is shot, and Hazleton becomes city manager.

3548 Escape of Squadron 32 of the Hruntan Navy from the Battle of Procyon. Founding of the Duchy of Gort.

3571 Interception of the war between Gort and Utopia.

3602 Reduction of Gort and Utopia by the Earth police. Second Hamiltonian Exodus. Death of Arpad Hrunta; dissolution of the Empire. Escape of Manhattan.

8

3844 The crossing of the Rift. First contact with the planet of He.

3850 The tipping of He; beginning of the first intergalactic crossing.

3900 Collapse of the germanium standard.

3905 Battle of the Jungle, in the Acolyte cluster. Lt. Lerner named Acolyte-Regent. Beginning of the March on Earth.

3910 Acolyte-Regent Lerner proclaims himself Emperor of Space.

3911 The flight of Hern VI. Annihilation of the Acolyte fleet by the Earth police. Death of Emperor Lerner, under an overdose of wisdom-weed, in a slum on Murphy.

3913 The Battle of Earth. Last stand of the Vegan Tyranny.

3917 Hern VI leaves the galaxy.

3918 Manhattan leaves the galaxy. Re-election of Mayor Amalfi.

3925 Passage of the anti-Okie bill.

3944 Discovery of the Interstellar Master Traders. Colonization of the Greater Magellanic Cloud.

3948 The Battle of the Blasted Heath. Destruction of IMT by the Earth police. Abandonment by Earth of the Clouds.

3949 Founding of New Earth.

4000 Assimilation by the Web of Hercules of the Earth culture; emergence of the Milky Way's IVth great civilization. The return of He.

4002 The Jehad of Jorn. Conquest and recovery of New Earth.

4004 The Ginnunga-Gap.

". . . While Vegan civilization was undergoing this peculiar decline in influence, while at the height of its political and military power, the culture which was eventually to replace it was beginning to unfold. The reader should bear in mind that at that time nobody had ever heard of the Earth, and the planet's sun, Sol, was known only as an undistinguished type Go star in the Draco sector. It is possible—although highly unlikely—that Vega knew that the Earth had developed space flight some time before the events we have just reviewed here. It was, however, only local interplanetary flight; up to this period, Earth had taken no part in Galactic history. It was inevitable, however, that Earth should make the two crucial discoveries which would bring it on to that starry stage. We may be very sure that Vega, had she known that Earth was to be her successor, would have exerted all of her enormous might to prevent it. That Vega failed to do so is evidence enough that she had no real idea of what was happening on Earth at this time. . . ."

—ACREFF-MONALES: *The Milky Way:*
Five Cultural Portraits

BOOK ONE

★

PRELUDE

The shadows flickered on the walls to his left and right, just inside the edges of his vision, like shapes stepping quickly back into invisible doorways. Despite his bone-deep weariness, they made him nervous, almost made him wish that Dr. Corsi would put out the fire. Nevertheless, he remained staring into the leaping orange light, feeling the heat tightening his cheeks and the skin around his eyes, and soaking into his chest.

Corsi stirred a little beside him, but Senator Wagoner's own weight on the sofa seemed to have been increasing ever since he had first sat down. He felt drained, lethargic, as old and heavy as a stone despite his forty-eight years; it had been a bad day in a long succession of bad days. Good days in Washington were the ones you slept through.

Next to him Corsi, for all that he was twenty years older, formerly Director of the Bureau of Standards, formerly Director of the World Health Organization, and presently head man of the American Association for the Advancement of Science (usually referred to in Washington as "the left-wing Triple-A-S"), felt as light and restless and quick as a chameleon.

"I suppose you know what a chance you're taking, coming to see me," Corsi said in his dry, whispery

13

voice. "I wouldn't be in Washington at all if I didn't think the interests of the AAAS required it. Not after the drubbing I've taken at MacHinery's hands. Even outside the government, it's like living in an aquarium —in a tank labelled 'Pirhana'. But you know about all that."

"I know," the senator agreed. The shadows jumped forward and retreated. "I was followed here myself. MacHinery's gumshoes have been trying to get something on me for a long time. But I had to talk to you, Seppi. I've done my best to understand everything I've found in the committee's files since I was made chairman—but a non-scientist has inherent limitations. And I didn't want to ask revealing questions of any of the boys on my staff. That would be a sure way to a leak—probably straight to MacHinery."

"That's the definition of a government expert these days," Corsi said, even more dryly. "A man of whom you don't dare ask an important question."

"Or who'll give you only the answer he thinks you want to hear," Wagoner said heavily. "I've hit that, too. Working for the government isn't a pink tea for a senator, either. Don't think I haven't wanted to be back in Alaska more than once; I've got a cabin on Kadiak where I can *enjoy* an open fire, without wondering if the shadows it throws carry notebooks. But that's enough self-pity. I ran for the office and I mean to be good at it, as good as I can be, anyhow."

"Which is good enough," Corsi said unexpectedly, taking the brandy snifter out of Wagoner's lax hand and replenishing the little amber lake at the bottom of it. The vapours came welling up over his cupped hand, heavy and rich. "Bliss, when I first heard that the Joint Congressional Committee on Space Flight was going to

14

fall into the hands of a freshman senator, one who'd been nothing but a press agent before his election——"

"Please," Wagoner said, wincing with mock tenderness. "A public relations counsel."

"As you like. Still and all, I turned the air blue. I knew it wouldn't have happened if any senator with seniority had wanted the committee, and the fact that none of them did seemed to me to be the worst indictment of the present Congress anyone could ask for. Every word I said was taken down, of course, and will be used against you, sooner or later. It's already been used against me, and thank God *that's* over. But I was wrong about you. You've done a whale of a good job; you've learned like magic. So if you want to cut your political throat by asking me for advice, then by God I'll give it to you."

Corsi thrust the snifter back into Wagoner's hand with something more than mock fury. "That goes for you, and for nobody else," he added. "I wouldn't tell anybody else in government the best way to pound sand —not unless the AAAS asked me to."

"I know you wouldn't, Seppi. That's part of our trouble. Thanks, anyhow." He swirled the brandy reflectively. "All right, then, tell me this: What's the matter with space flight?"

"The Army," Corsi said promptly.

"Yes, but that's not all. Not by a long shot. Sure, the Army Space Service is graft-ridden, shot through with jealousy, and gone rigid in the brains. But it was far worse back in the days when half a dozen branches of government were working on space-flight at the same time—the Weather Bureau, the Navy, your bureau, the Air Force and so on. I've seen some documents dating back that far. The Earth Satellite Programme was announced in 1944; we didn't actually get SV-1 up there until 1962, after the Army was given full jurisdiction. They couldn't even get the damned thing off the drawing boards; every Rear-Admiral insisted that the plans include a parking place for his pet launch. At least now we *have* space-flight.

"But there's something far more radically wrong now. If space flight were still a live proposition, by now some of it would have been taken away from the Army again. There'd be some merchant shipping, maybe; or even small passenger lines for the luxury trade, for the kind of people who'll go in uncomfortable ways to unliveable places just because it's horribly expensive." He chuckled heavily. "Like fox-hunting in England a hundred years ago; some Irish senator, Gogarty I think it was, called it 'the pursuit of the inedible by the unspeakable'."

"Isn't it still a little early for that?" Corsi said.

"In 2013? I don't think so. But if I'm rushing us on that one point, I can mention others. Why have there been no major exploratory expeditions for the past fifteen years? I should have thought that as soon as that tenth planet, Proserpine, was discovered, some university or foundation would have wanted to go there. It has a big fat moon that would make a fine base—no weather exists at those temperatures—there's no sun in the sky out there to louse up photographic plates, it's only another zero-magnitude star—and so on. That kind of thing used to be meat and drink to private explorers. Given a millionaire with a thirst for science, like old Hale, and a sturdy organizer with a little grandstand in him—a Byrd-type—and we should have had a Proserpine Two station long ago. Yet space has been dead since Titan Station was set up in 1981. Why?"

16

He watched the flames a moment.

"Then", he said, "there's the whole question of invention in the field. It's stopped, Seppi. Stopped cold."

Corsi said: "I seem to remember a paper from the boys on Titan not so long ago——"

"On xenobacteriology. Sure. That's not space flight, Seppi; space flight only made it possible; their results don't update space flight itself, don't improve it, make it more attractive. Those guys aren't even interested in it. *Nobody* is any more. That's why it's stopped changing.

"For instance: we're still using ion-rockets, driven by an atomic pile. It works, and there are a thousand minor variations on the principle; but the principle itself was described by Coupling in 1954! Think of it, Seppi—not one single new, basic engine design in *fifty years!* And what about hull design? That's still based on von Braun's work—older even than Coupling's. Is it really possible that there's nothing better than those frameworks of hitched onions? Or those powered gliders that act as ferries for them? Yet I can't find anything in the committee's files that looks any better."

"Are you sure you'd know a minor change from a major one?"

"You be the judge," Wagoner said grimly. "The hottest thing in current spaceship design is a new elliptically wound spring for acceleration couches. It drags like a leaf-spring with gravity, and pushes like a coil-spring against it. The design wastes energy in one direction, stores it in the other. At last reports, couches made with it feel like sacks stuffed with green tomatoes, but we think we'll have the bugs worked out of it soon. Tomato bugs, I suppose. Top Secret."

"There's one more Top Secret I'm not supposed to know," Corsi said. "Luckily it'll be no trouble to forget."

"All right, try this one. We have a new water-bottle for ships' stores. It's made of aluminium foil, to be collapsed from the bottom like a toothpaste tube to feed the water into the man's mouth."

"But a plastic membrane collapsed by air-pressure is handier, weighs less——"

"Sure it does. And this foil tube is already standard for paste rations. All that's new about this thing is the proposal that we use it for water too. The proposal came to us from a lobbyist for CanAm Metals, with strong endorsements by a couple of senators from the Pacific north-west. You can guess what we did with it."

"I am beginning to see your drift."

"Then I'll wind it up as fast as I can," Wagoner said. "What it all comes to is that the whole structure of space flight as it stands now is creaking, obsolescent, over-elaborate, decaying. The field is static; no, worse than that, it's losing ground. By this time, our ships ought to be sleeker and faster, and able to carry bigger payloads. We ought to have done away with this dichotomy between ships that can land on a planet, and ships that can fly from one planet to another.

"The whole question of *using* the planets for something—something, that is, besides research—ought to be within sight of settlement. Instead, nobody even discusses it any more. And our chances to settle it grow worse every year. Our appropriations are dwindling, as it gets harder and harder to convince the Congress that space flight is really good for anything. You can't sell the Congress on the long-range rewards of basic research, anyhow; Representatives have to stand for election every two years, Senators every six years; that's just about as far ahead as most of them are prepared to look. And suppose we tried to explain to them the basic research we're doing? We couldn't; it's classified!

"And above all, Seppi—this may be only my personal ignorance speaking, but if so, I'm stuck with it—above all, I think that by now we ought to have some slight clue toward an inter*stellar* drive. We ought even to have a model, no matter how crude—as crude as a Fourth-of-July rocket compared to a Coupling engine, but with the principle visible. But we don't. As a matter of fact, we've written off the stars. Nobody I can talk to thinks we'll ever reach them."

Corsi got up and walked lightly to the window, where he stood with his back to the room, as though trying to look through the light-tight blind down on to the deserted street. While he stood there, a shot blatted not far away, and the echoes bounded back at them from the face of the embassy across the street. It was not a common sound in Washington, but neither was it unusual: it was almost surely one of the city's thousands of anonymous snoopers firing at a counter-agent, a cop, or a shadow.

Corsi made no responding movement. To Wagoner's fire-hazed eyes, he was scarcely more than a shadow himself. The senator found himself thinking, for perhaps the twentieth time in the past six months, that Corsi might even be glad to be out of it all, branded unreliable though he was. Then, again for at least the twentieth time, Wagoner remembered the repeated clearance hearings, the oceans of dubious testimony and gossip from witnesses with no faces or names, the clamour in the press when Corsi was found to have roomed in college with a man suspected of being an ex-YPSL member, the denunciation on the Senate floor by one of MacHinery's captive solons, more hearings, the endless barrage of vilification and hatred, the letters beginning "Dear Doctor Corsets, You bum," and signed "True American". . . . To get out of it that way was worse than enduring it, no matter how stoutly most of your fellow scholars stood by you afterwards.

"I shan't be the first to say so to you," the physicist said, turning at last. "I don't think we'll ever reach the stars either, Bliss. And I am not very conservative, as physicists go. We just don't live long enough for us to become a star-travelling race. A mortal man limited to speeds below that of light is as unsuited to interstellar travel as a moth would be to crossing the Atlantic. I'm sorry to believe that, certainly; but I do believe it."

Wagoner nodded and filed the speech away. On that subject, he had expected even less than Corsi had given him.

"But", Corsi said, lifting his snifter from the table, "it isn't impossible that inter*planetary* flight could be bettered. I agree with you that it's rotting away now. I'd suspected that it might be, and your showing to-night is conclusive."

"Then why is it happening?" Wagoner demanded.

"Because scientific method doesn't work any more."

"*What!* Excuse me, Seppi, but that's sort of like hearing an Archbishop say that Christianity doesn't work any more. What do you mean?"

Corsi smiled sourly. "Perhaps I was overdramatic. But it's true that, under present conditions, scientific method is a blind alley. It depends on freedom of information, and we deliberately killed that. In my bureau, when it was mine, we seldom knew who was working on what project at any given time; we seldom knew whether or not somebody else in the bureau was duplicating it; we never knew whether or not some other

20

department might be duplicating it. All we could be sure of was that many men, working in similar fields, were stamping their results *Secret* because that was the easy way—not only to keep the work out of Russian hands, but to keep the workers in the clear if their own government should investigate them. How can you apply scientific method to a problem when you're forbidden to see the data?

"Then there's the calibre of scientist we have working for the government now. The few first-rate men we have are so harassed by the security set-up—and by the constant suspicion that's focused on them because they *are* top men in their fields, and hence anything they might leak would be particularly valuable—that it takes them years to solve what used to be very simple problems. As for the rest—well, our staff at Standards consisted almost entirely of third-raters: some of them were very dogged and patient men indeed, but low on courage and even lower on imagination. They spent all their time operating mechanically by the cook-book— the routine of scientific method—and had less to show for it every year."

"Everything you've said could be applied to the space-flight research that's going on now, without changing a comma," Wagoner said. "But Seppi, if scientific method used to be sound, it should still be sound. It ought to work for anybody, even third-raters. Why has it suddenly turned sour now—after centuries of unbroken successes?"

"The time lapse", Corsi said sombrely, "is of the first importance. Remember, Bliss, that scientific method is *not* a natural law. It doesn't exist in nature, but only in our heads; in short, it's a way of thinking about things —a way of sifting evidence. It was bound to become

21

obsolescent sooner or later, just as sorites and paradigms and syllogisms became obsolete before it. Scientific method works fine while there are thousands of obvious facts lying about for the taking—facts as obvious and measurable as how fast a stone falls, or what the order of the colours is in a rainbow. But the more subtle the facts to be discovered become—the more they retreat into the realms of the invisible, the intangible, the unweighable, the sub-microscopic, the abstract— the more expensive and time-consuming it is to investigate them by scientific method.

"And when you reach a stage where the *only* research worth doing costs millions of dollars per experiment, then those experiments can be paid for only by government. Governments can make the best use only of third-rate men, men who can't leaven the instructions in the cook-book with the flashes of insight you need to make basic discoveries. The result is what you see: sterility, stasis, dry rot."

"Then what's left?" Wagoner said. "What are we going to do now? I know you well enough to suspect that you're not giving up all hope."

"No," Corsi said, "I haven't given up, but I'm quite helpless to change the situation you're complaining about. After all, I'm on the outside. Which is probably good for me." He paused, and then said suddenly: "There's no hope of getting the government to drop the security system completely?"

"Completely?"

"Nothing else would do."

"No," Wagoner said. "Not even partially, I'm afraid. Not any longer."

Corsi sat down and leaned forward, his elbows on his knobby knees, staring into the dying coals. "Then I have two pieces of advice to give you, Bliss. Actually they're two sides of the same coin. First of all, begin by abandoning these multi-million-dollar, Manhattan-District approaches. We don't need a newer, still finer measurement of electron resonance one-tenth so badly as we need new pathways, new categories of knowledge. The colossal research project is defunct; what we need now is pure skullwork."

"From *my* staff?"

"From wherever you can get it. That's the other half of my recommendation. If I were you, I would go to the crackpots."

Wagoner waited. Corsi said these things for effect; he liked drama, in small doses. He would explain in a moment.

"Of course I don't mean total crackpots," Corsi said. "But you'll have to draw the line yourself. You need marginal contributors, scientists of good reputation generally whose obsessions don't strike fire with other members of their profession. Like the Crehore atom, or old Ehrenhaft's theory of magnetic currents, or the Milne cosmology—you'll have to find the fruitful one yourself. Look for discards, and then find out whether or not the idea deserved to be *totally* discarded. And— don't accept the first 'expert' opinion that you get."

"Winnow chaff, in other words."

"What else is there to winnow?" Corsi said. "Of course it's a long chance, but you can't turn to scientists of real stature now; it's too late for that. Now you'll have to use sports, freaks, near-misses."

"Starting where?"

"Oh," said Corsi, "how about gravity? I don't know any other subject that's attracted a greater quota of idiot speculations. Yet the acceptable theories of what

23

gravity is are of no practical use to us. They can't be put to work to help lift a spaceship. We can't manipulate gravity as a field; we don't even have a set of equations for it that we can agree upon. No more will we find such a set by spending fortunes and decades on the project. The law of diminishing returns has washed that approach out."

Wagoner got up. "You don't leave me much," he said glumly.

"No," Corsi agreed. "I leave you only what you started with. That's more than most of us are left with, Bliss."

Wagoner grinned tightly at him and the two men shook hands. As Wagoner left, he saw Corsi again silhouetted against the fire, his back to the door, his shoulders bent. The senator closed the door quietly.

He was shadowed all the way back to his own apartment, but this time he hardly noticed. He was thinking about an immortal man who flew from star to star faster than light.

1

The parade of celebrities, notorieties, and just plain
brass that passed through the reception-room of Jno.
Pfitzner & Sons, Inc., was marvellous to behold. During the hour and a half that Col. Paige Russell had been
cooling his heels, he had identified the following
publicity-saints:

Senator Bliss Wagoner (Dem., Alaska), chairman of
the Joint Congressional Committee on Space Flight;

Dr. Guiseppi Corsi, president of the American
Association for the Advancement of Science, and a
former Director of the World Health Organization; and,

Francis Xavier MacHinery, hereditary head of the
FBI.

He had seen also a number of other notables, of
lesser calibre, but whose business at a firm which made
biologicals was an equally improper subject for guessing
games. He fidgeted.

At the present moment, the girl at the desk was talking softly with a seven-star general, which was a rank
nearly as high as a man could rise in the Army. The
general was so preoccupied that he had failed completely to recognize Paige's salute. He was passed
through swiftly. One of the two swinging doors with the
glass ports let into them moved outward behind the
desk, and Paige caught a glimpse of a stocky, dark-

haired, pleasant-faced man in a conservative grosse-pointilliste suit.

"Gen. Horsefield, glad to see you. Come in."

The door closed, leaving Paige once more with nothing to look at but the motto written over the entrance in German black-letter:

Wider den Tod ist kein Krautlein gewachsen!

Since he did not know the language, he had already translated this by the If-only-it-were-English system, which made it come out, "The fatter toad is waxing on the kine's cole-slaw." This did not seem to fit what little he knew about the eating habits of either animal, and it was certainly no fit admonition for workers in the main plant of the world's largest producers of biological drugs.

Of course, Paige could always look at the receptionist —but after an hour and a half he had about plumbed the uttermost depths of that ecstasy. The girl was pretty in a way, but hardly striking, even to a recently returned spaceman. Perhaps if someone would yank those black-rimmed pixie glasses away from her and undo that bun at the back of her head, she might pass, at least in the light of a whale-oil lamp in an igloo during a record blizzard.

This too was odd now that he thought about it. A firm as large as Pfitzner could have its pick of the glossiest of office girls, especially these days.

All in all, Paige was thoroughly well past mere mild annoyance with being stalled. He was, after all, here at these people's specific request, doing them a small favour for which they had asked him—and soaking up good leave-time in the process. Abruptly he got up and strode to the desk.

"Excuse me, miss," he said, "but I think you're being

26

goddamned impolite. As a matter of fact, I'm beginning to think you people are making a fool of me. Do you want these, or don't you?"

He unbuttoned his right breast pocket and pulled out three little pliofilm packets, heat-sealed to plastic mailing tags. Each packet contained a small spoonful of dirt. The tags were addressed to Jno. Pfitzner & Sons, Inc., The Bronx 153, WPO 249920, Earth; and each carried a $25 rocket-mail stamp for which Pfitzner had paid, still uncancelled.

"Colonel Russell, I agree with you," the girl said, looking up at him seriously. She looked even less glamorous than she had at a distance, but she did have a pert and interesting nose, and the current royal-purple lip-shade suited her better than it did most of the novalettes to be seen on 3–V these days. "It's just that you've caught us on a very bad day. We do want the samples, of course. They're very important to us, otherwise we wouldn't have put you to the trouble of collecting them for us."

"Then why can't I give them to someone?"

"You could give them to me," the girl suggested gently. "I'll pass them along faithfully, I promise you."

Paige shook his head. "Not after this run-around. I did just what your firm asked me to do, and I'm here to see the results. I picked up soils from every one of my ports of call, even when it was a nuisance to do it. I mailed in a lot of them; these are only the last of a series. Do you know where these bits of dirt came from?"

"I'm sorry, it's slipped my mind. It's been a very busy day."

"Two of them are from Ganymede; and the other one is from Jupiter V, right in the shadow of the Bridge gang's shack. The normal temperature on both satellites is about two hundred degrees below Fahrenheit zero. Ever try to swing a pick against ground frozen that solid—working inside a spacesuit? But I got the dirt for you. Now I want to see why Pfitzner wants dirt."

The girl shrugged. "I'm sure you were told why before you even left Earth."

"Supposing I was? I know that you people get drugs out of dirt. But aren't the guys who bring in the samples entitled to see how the process works? What if Pfitzner gets some new wonder-drug out of one of my samples—couldn't I have a sentence or two of explanation to pass on to my kids?"

The swinging doors bobbed open, and the affable face of the stocky man was thrust into the room.

"Dr. Abbott not here yet, Anne?" he said.

"Not yet, Mr. Gunn. I'll call you the minute he arrives."

"But you'll keep me sitting at least another ninety minutes," Paige said flatly. Gunn looked him over, starting at the colonel's eagle on his collar and stopping at the winged crescent pinned over his pocket.

"Apologies, Colonel, but we're having ourselves a small crisis today," he said, smiling tentatively. "I gather you've brought us some samples from space. If you could possibly come back tomorrow, I'd be happy to give you all the time in the world. But right now——"

Gunn ducked his head in apology and pulled it in, as though he had just cuckooed 2400 and had to go somewhere and lie down until 0100. Just before the door came to rest behind him, a faint but unmistakable sound slipped through it.

Somewhere in the laboratories of Jno. Pfitzner & Sons, Inc. a baby was crying.

Paige listened, blinking, until the sound was damped off. When he looked back down at the desk again, the expression of the girl behind it seemed distinctly warier.

"Look," he said. "I'm not asking a great favour of you. I don't want to know anything I shouldn't know. All I want to know is how you plan to process my packets of soil. It's just simple curiosity—backed up by a trip that covered a few hundred millions of miles. Am I entitled to know for my trouble, or not?"

"You are and you aren't," the girl said steadily. "We want your samples, and we'll agree that they're unusually interesting to us because they came from the Jovian system—the first such that we've ever gotten. But that's no guarantee that we'll find anything useful in them."

"It isn't?"

"No. Colonel Russell, you're not the first man to come here with soil samples, believe me. We've asked virtually every space-pilot, every Witness missionary, every commercial traveller, every explorer, every foreign correspondent to scoop up soil samples for us, wherever they may go. Before we discovered ascomycin, we had to screen *one hundred thousand* soil samples, including several hundred from Mars and nearly five thousand from the Moon. And do you know where we found the organism that produces ascomycin? On an over-ripe peach one of our detail men picked up from a peddler's stall in Baltimore!"

"I see the point," Paige said reluctantly. "What's ascomycin, by the way?"

The girl looked down at her desk and moved a piece of paper from *here* to *there*. "It's a new antibiotic," she said. "We'll be marketing it soon. But I could tell you the same kind of story about other such drugs."

"I see." Paige was not quite sure he did see, however, after all. He had heard the name of Pfitzner fall from some very unlikely lips during his many months in space. As far as he had been able to determine after he had become sensitized to the sound, about every third person on the planets was either collecting samples for the firm or knew somebody who was. The grapevine, which among spacemen was the only trusted medium of communication, had it that the company was doing important government work. That, of course, was nothing unusual in the Age of Defence, but Paige had heard enough to suspect that Pfitzner was something special —something as big, perhaps, as the historic Manhattan District and at least twice as secret.

The door opened and emitted Gunn for the third time hand-running, this time all the way.

"Not yet?" he said to the girl. "Evidently he isn't going to make it. Unfortunate. But I've some spare time now, Colonel——"

"Russell, Paige Russell, Army Space Corps."

"Thank you. If you'll accept my apologies for our preoccupation, Colonel Russell, I'll be glad to show you around our little establishment. My name, by the way, is Truman Gunn, vice-president in charge of exports."

"I'm importing at the moment," Paige said, holding out the soil samples. Gunn took them reverently and dropped them in a pocket of his jacket. "But I'd enjoy seeing the labs."

He nodded to the girl and the doors closed between them. He was inside.

The place was at least as fascinating as he had expected it to be. Gunn showed him, first, the rooms where the incoming samples were classified and then distributed to the laboratories proper. In the first of these, a measured fraction of a sample was dropped into a one-litre flask of sterile distilled water, swirled to distribute it evenly, and then passed through a series of dilutions. The final suspensions were then used to inoculate test-tube slants and petri plates containing a wide variety of nutrient media, which went into the incubator.

"In the next lab here—Dr. Aquino isn't in at the moment, so we mustn't touch anything, but you can see through the glass quite clearly—we transfer from the plates and agar slants to a new set of media," Gunn explained. "But here each organism found in the sample has a set of cultures of its own, so that if it secretes anything into one of the media, that something won't be contaminated."

"If it does, the amount must be very tiny," Paige said. "How do you detect it?"

"Directly, by its action. Do you see the rows of plates with the white paper discs in their centres, and the four furrows in the agar radiating from the discs? Well, each one of those furrows is impregnated with culture medium from one of the pure cultures. If all four streaks grow thriving bacterial colonies, then the medium on the paper disc contains no antibiotic against those four germs. If one or more of the streaks fails to grow, or is retarded compared to the others, then we have hope."

In the succeeding laboratory, antibiotics which had been found by the disc method were pitted against a whole spectrum of dangerous organisms. About 90 per cent of the discoveries were eliminated here, Gunn explained, either because they were insufficiently active or because they duplicated the antibiotic spectra of already known drugs. "What we call 'insufficiently active' varies with the circumstances, however," he

31

added. "An antibiotic which shows *any* activity against tuberculosis or against Hansen's disease—leprosy—is always of interest to us, even if it attacks no other germ at all."

A few antibiotics which passed their spectrum tests went on to a miniature pilot plant, where the organisms that produced them were set to work in a deep-aerated fermentation tank. From this bubbling liquor, comparatively large amounts of the crude drug were extracted, purified, and sent to the pharmacology lab for tests on animals.

"We lose a lot of otherwise promising antibiotics here, too," Gunn said. "Most of them turn out to be too toxic to be used in—or even on—the human body. We've had Hansen's bacillus knocked out a thousand times in the test-tube, only to find here that the antibiotic is much more quickly fatal *in vivo* than is leprosy itself. But once we're sure that the drug isn't toxic, or that its toxicity is outweighed by its therapeutic efficacy, it goes out of our shop entirely, to hospitals and to individual doctors for clinical trial. We also have a virology lab in Vermont where we test our new drugs against virus diseases like the 'flu and polio—it isn't safe to operate such a lab in a large city like The Bronx."

"It's much more elaborate than I would have imagined," Paige said. "But I can see that it's well worth the trouble. Did you work out this sample-screening technique here?"

"Oh, my, no," Gunn said, smiling indulgently. "Waksman, the discoverer of streptomycin, laid down the essential procedure decades ago. We aren't even the first firm to use it on a large scale; one of our competitors did that, and found a broad-spectrum antibiotic called chloramphenicol with it, scarcely a year after they'd begun. That was what convinced the rest of us that we'd better adopt the technique, before we got shut out of the market entirely. A good thing, too; otherwise we'd none of us have discovered tetracycline, which turned out to be the most versatile antibiotic ever tested."

Farther down the corridor a door opened. The squall of a baby came out of it, much louder than before. It was not the sustained crying of a child who had had a year or so to practise, but the short-breathed "ah-la, ah-la, ah-la" of a newborn infant.

Paige raised his eyebrows. "Is that one of your experimental animals?"

"Ha, ha," Gunn said. "We're enthusiasts in this business, Colonel, but we must draw the line somewhere. No, one of our technicians has a baby-sitting problem, and so we've given her permission to bring the child to work with her, until she's worked out a better solution."

Paige had to admit that Gunn thought fast on his feet. That story had come reeling out of him like so much ticker tape, without the slightest sign of a preliminary double-take. It was not Gunn's fault that Paige, who had been through a marriage which had lasted five years before he had taken to space, could distinguish the cry of a baby old enough to be out of a hospital nursery from that of one only days old.

"Isn't this", Paige said, "a rather dangerous place to park an infant—with so many disease germs, poisonous disinfectants, and such things all around?"

"Oh, we take all proper precautions. I daresay our staff has a lower yearly sickness rate than you'll find in industrial plants of comparable size, simply because we're more aware of the problem. Now if we go through

c   33

this door, Colonel Russell, we'll see the final step, the main plant where we turn out drugs in quantity after they've proved themselves."

"Yes, I'd like that. Do you have ascomycin in production now?"

This time, Gunn looked at him sharply and without any attempt to disguise his interest. "No," he said, "that's still out on clinical trial. May I ask you, Colonel Russell, just how you happened to——"

The question, which Paige realized belatedly would have been rather sticky to answer, never did get all the way asked. Over Truman Gunn's head, a squawk-box said, "Mr. Gunn, Dr. Abbott has just arrived."

Gunn turned away from the door that, he had said, led out to the main plant, with just the proper modicum of polite regret. "There's my man," he said. "I'm afraid I'm going to have to cut this tour short, Colonel Russell. You may have seen what a collection of important people we have in the plant today; we've been waiting only for Dr. Abbott to begin a very important meeting. If you'll oblige me——"

Paige could say nothing but: "Certainly." After what seemed only a few seconds, Gunn deposited him smoothly in the reception room from which he had started.

"Did you see what you wanted to see?" the receptionist said.

"I think so," Paige said thoughtfully. "Except that what I wanted to see sort of changed in mid-flight. Miss Anne, I have a petition to put before you. Would you be kind enough to have dinner with me this evening?"

"No," the girl said. "I've seen quite a few spacemen, Colonel Russell, and I'm no longer impressed. Further-

34

more, I shan't tell you anything you haven't heard from Mr. Gunn, so there's no need for you to spend your money or your leave-time on me. Good-bye."

"Not so fast," Paige said. "I mean business—or, if you like, I mean to make trouble. If you've met spacemen before, you know that they like to be independent —not much like the conformists who never leave the ground. I'm not after your maidenly laughter, either. I'm after information."

"Not interested," the girl said. "Save your breath."

"MacHinery is here," Paige said quietly. "So is Senator Wagoner, and some other people who have influence. Suppose I should collar any one of those people and accuse Pfitzner of conducting human vivisection?"

That told: Paige could see the girl's knuckles whitening. "You don't know what you're talking about," she said.

"That's my complaint. And I take it seriously. There were some things Mr. Gunn wasn't able to conceal from me, though he tried very hard. Now, am I going to put my suspicions through channels—and get Pfitzner investigated—or would you rather be sociable, over a fine flounder broiled in paprika butter?"

The look she gave him back was one of almost pure hatred. She seemed able to muster no other answer. The expression did not at all suit her; as a matter of fact, she looked less like someone he would want to date than any other girl he could remember. Why *should* he spend his money or his leave-time on her? There were, after all, about five millions of surplus women in the United States by the Census of 2000, and at least 4,999,950 of them must be prettier and less recalcitrant than this one.

"All right," she said abruptly. "Your natural charm

35

has swept me off my feet, Colonel. For the record, there's no other reason for my acceptance. It would be even funnier to call your bluff and see how far you'd get with that vivisection tale, but I don't care to tie my company up in a personal joke."

"Good enough," Paige said, uncomfortably aware that his bluff in fact *had* been called. "Suppose I pick you up——"

He broke off, suddenly noticing that voices were rising behind the double doors. An instant later, General Horsefield bulled into the reception room, closely followed by Gunn.

"I want it clearly understood, once and for all," Horsefield was rumbling, "that this entire project is going to wind up under military control unless we can show results before it's time to ask for a new appropriation. There's still a lot going on here that the Pentagon will regard as piddling inefficiency and highbrow theorizing. And if that's what the Pentagon reports, you know what the Treasury will do—or Congress will do it for them. We're going to have to cut back, Gunn. Understand? Cut right back to basics!"

"General, we're as far back to basics as we possibly can get," Truman Gunn said, placatingly enough, but with considerable firmness as well. "We're not going to put a gram of that drug into production until we're satisfied with it on all counts. Any other course would be suicide."

"You know I'm on your side," Horsefield said, his voice becoming somewhat less threatening. "So is General Alsos, for that matter. But this is a war we're fighting, whether the public understands it or not. And on as sensitive a matter as these death-dopes, we can't afford——"

36

Gunn, who had spotted Paige belatedly at the conclusion of his own speech, had been signalling Horsefield ever since with his eyebrows, and suddenly it took. The general swung around and glared at Paige, who, since he was uncovered now, was relieved of the necessity for saluting. Despite the sudden freezing silence, it was evident that Gunn was trying to retain in his manner toward Paige some shreds of professional cordiality—a courtesy which Paige was not too sure he merited, considering the course his conversation with the girl had taken.

As for Horsefield, he relegated Paige to the ghetto of "unauthorized persons" with a single look. Paige had no intention of remaining in that classification for a second longer than it would take him to get out of it, preferably without having been asked his name; it was deadly dangerous. With a mumbled "—at eight, then," to the girl, Paige sidled ingloriously out of the Pfitzner reception room and beat it.

He was, he reflected later in the afternoon before his shaving mirror, subjecting himself to an extraordinary series of small humiliations, to get closer to a matter which was none of his business. Worse: it was obviously Top Secret, which made it potentially lethal even for everyone authorized to know about it, let alone for rank snoopers. In the Age of Defence, to know was to be suspect, in the West as in the USSR; the two great nation-complexes had been becoming more and more alike in their treatment of "security" for the past fifty years. It had even been a mistake to mention the Bridge on Jupiter to the girl—for despite the fact that everyone knew that the Bridge existed, anyone who spoke of it with familiarity could quickly earn the label of being dangerously flap-jawed. Especially if the speaker, like Paige, had actually been stationed in the Jovian system for a while, whether he had had access to information about the Bridge or not.

And especially if the talker, like Paige, had actually spoken to the Bridge gang, worked with them on marginal projects, was known to have talked to Charity Dillon, the Bridge foreman. More especially if he held military rank, making it possible for him to sell security files to Congressmen, the traditional way of advancing a military career ahead of normal promotion schedules.

And most especially if the man was discovered nosing about a new and different classified project, one to which he hadn't even been assigned.

Why, after all, was he taking the risk? He didn't even know the substance of the matter; he was no biologist. To all outside eyes the Pfitzner project was simply another piece of research in antibiotics, and a rather routinized research project at that. Why should a spaceman like Paige find himself flying so close to the candle already?

He wiped the depilatory cream off his face into a paper towel, and saw his own eyes looking back at him from the concave mirror, as magnified as an owl's. The image, however, was only his own, despite the distortion. It gave him back no answer.

2

A screeching tornado was rocking the Bridge when
the alarm sounded; it was making the whole structure
shudder and sway. This was normal, and Robert Helmuth barely noticed it. There was always a tornado
shaking the Bridge. The whole planet was enswathed
in tornadoes, and worse.

The scanner on the foreman's board had given 114
as the sector where the trouble was. That was at the
north-western end of the Bridge, where it broke off,
leaving nothing but the raging clouds of ammonia crystals and methane, and a sheer drop thirty miles down
to the invisible surface. There were no ultraphone
"eyes" at that end to show a general view of the area—
in so far as any general view was possible—because both
ends of the Bridge were incomplete.

With a sigh, Helmuth put the beetle into motion. The
little car, as flat-bottomed and thin through as a bed-
bug, got slowly under way on its ball-bearing races,
guided and held firmly to the surface of the Bridge by
ten close-set flanged rails. Even so, the hydrogen gales
made a terrific siren-like shrieking between the edge of
the vehicle and the deck, and the impact of the falling
drops of ammonia upon the curved roof was as heavy
and deafening as a rain of cannon balls. As a matter of
fact, the drops weighed almost as much as cannon-balls

here under Jupiter's two-and-a-half-fold gravity, although they were not much bigger than ordinary raindrops. Every so often, too, there was a blast, accompanied by a dull orange glare, which made the car, the deck, and the Bridge itself buck savagely; even a small shock wave travelled through the incredibly dense atmosphere of the planet like the armour-plate of a bursting battleship.

These blasts were below, however, on the surface. While they shook the structure of the Bridge heavily, they almost never interfered with its functioning. And they could not, in the very nature of things, do Helmuth any harm.

Helmuth, after all, was not on Jupiter—though that was becoming harder and harder for him to bear in mind. Nobody was on Jupiter; had any real damage ever been done to the Bridge, it probably would never have been repaired. There was nobody on Jupiter to repair it; only the machines which were themselves part of the Bridge.

The Bridge was building itself. Massive, alone, and lifeless, it grew in the black deeps of Jupiter.

It had been well planned. From Helmuth's point of view—that of the scanners on the beetle—almost nothing could be seen of it, for the beetle tracks ran down the centre of the deck, and in the darkness and perpetual storm even ultrawave-assisted vision could not penetrate more than a few hundred yards at the most. The width of the Bridge, which no one would ever see, was eleven miles; its height, as incomprehensible to the Bridge gang as a skyscraper to an ant, thirty miles; its length, deliberately unspecified in the plans, fifty-four miles at the moment and still increasing—a squat, colossal structure, built with engineering principles, methods, materials and tools never touched before now. . . .

For the very good reason that they would have been impossible anywhere else. Most of the Bridge, for instance, was made of ice: a marvellous structural material under a pressure of a million atmospheres, at a temperature of 94 degrees below Fahrenheit zero. Under such conditions, the best structural steel is a friable, talc-like powder, and aluminium becomes a peculiar transparent substance that splits at a tap; water, on the other hand, becomes Ice IV, a dense, opaque white medium which will deform to a heavy stress, but will break only under impacts huge enough to lay whole Earthly cities waste. Never mind that it took millions of megawatts of power to keep the Bridge up and growing every hour of the day; the winds on Jupiter blow at velocities up to twenty-five thousand miles per hour, and will never stop blowing, as they may have been blowing for more than four billion years; there is power enough.

Back home, Helmuth remembered, there had been talk of starting another Bridge on Saturn, and perhaps, later still, on Uranus too. But that had been politicians' talk. The Bridge was almost five thousand miles below the visible surface of Jupiter's atmosphere—luckily in a way, for at the top of that atmosphere the temperature was 76 Fahrenheit degrees colder than it was down by the Bridge, but even with that differential the Bridge's mechanisms were just barely manageable. The bottom of Saturn's atmosphere, if the radiosonde readings could be trusted, was just 16,878 miles below the top of the Saturnian clouds one could see through the telescope, and the temperature down there was below $-150°$ C. Under those conditions, even pressure-ice would be

41

immovable, and could not be worked with anything softer than itself.

And as for a Bridge on Uranus. . . . As far as Helmuth was concerned, Jupiter was quite bad enough.

The beetle crept within sight of the end of the Bridge and stopped automatically. Helmuth set the vehicle's "eyes" for highest penetration, and examined the nearby I-beams.

The great bars were as close-set as screening. They had to be, in order to support even their own weight, let alone the weight of the components of the Bridge. The gravity down here was two and a half times as great as Earth's.

Even under that load, the whole webwork of girders was flexing and fluctuating to the harpist-fingered gale. It had been designed to do that, but Helmuth could never help being alarmed by the movement. Habit alone assured him that he had nothing to fear from it.

He took the automatic cut-out out of the circuit and inched the beetle forward on manual control. This was only Sector 113, and the Bridge's own Wheatstone scanning system—there was no electronic device anywhere on the Bridge, since it was impossible to maintain a vacuum on Jupiter—said that the trouble was in Sector 114. The boundary of that sector was still fully fifty feet away.

It was a bad sign. Helmuth scratched nervously in his red beard. Evidently there was cause for alarm—real alarm, not just the deep grinding depression which he always felt while working on the Bridge. Any damage serious enough to halt the beetle a full sector short of the trouble area was bound to be major.

It might even turn out to be the disaster which he had felt lurking ahead of him ever since he had been made foreman of the Bridge—that disaster which the Bridge itself could not repair, sending man reeling home from Jupiter in defeat.

The secondaries cut in, and the beetle hunkered down once more against the deck, the ball-bearings on which it rode frozen magnetically to the rails. Grimly, Helmuth cut the power to the magnet windings and urged the flat craft inch by inch across the danger line.

Almost at once, the car tilted just perceptibly to the left, and the screaming of the winds between its edges and the deck shot up the scale, sirening in and out of the soundless-dogwhistle range with an eeriness which set Helmuth's teeth on edge. The beetle itself fluttered and chattered like an alarm-clock hammer between the surface of the deck and the flanges of the tracks.

Ahead there was still nothing to be seen but the horizontal driving of the clouds and the hail, roaring along the length of the Bridge, out of the blackness into the beetle's fanlights, and onward into blackness again toward the horizon which, like the Bridge itself, no eye would ever see.

Thirty miles below, the fusillade of hydrogen explosions continued. Evidently something really wild was going on on the surface. Helmuth could not remember having heard so much vulcanism in years.

There was a flat, especially heavy crash, and a long line of fuming orange fire came pouring down the seething air into the depths, feathering horizontally like the mane of a Lipizzan stallion, directly in front of Helmuth. Instinctively, he winced and drew back from the board, although that stream of flame actually was only a little less cold than the rest of the storming, streaming gases, and far too cold to injure the Bridge.

In the momentary glare, however, he saw something:

an upward twisting of shadows, patterned but obviously unfinished, fluttering in silhouette against the lurid light of the hydrogen cataract.

The end of the Bridge.

Wrecked.

Helmuth grunted involuntarily and backed the beetle away. The flare dimmed; the light poured down the sky and fell away into the raging sea of liquid hydrogen thirty miles below. The scanner clucked with satisfaction as the beetle recrossed the danger line into Sector 113.

Helmuth turned the body of the vehicle 180 degrees on its chassis, presenting its back to the dying orange torrent. There was nothing further that he could do at the moment on the Bridge. He searched his control board—a ghost image of which was cast on the screen across the scene on the Bridge—for the blue button marked *Garage*, punched it savagely, and tore off his foreman's helmet.

Obediently, the Bridge vanished.

*
* 3 *

The girl—whose full name, Paige found, was Anne
Abbott—looked moderately acceptable in her summer
suit, on the left lapel of which she wore a model of the
tetracycline molecule with the atoms picked out in tiny
synthetic gems. But she was even less inclined to talk
when he picked her up than she had been in Pfitzner's
reception room. Paige himself had never been expert at
making small talk, and in the face of her obvious, con-
tinuing resentment, his parched spring of social invention went underground completely.

Five minutes later, all talk became impossible, anyhow. The route to the restaurant Paige had chosen lay
across Foley Square, where there turned out to be a
Witness Mission going. The Caddy Paige had hired—
at nearly a quarter of his leave-pay, for commercial
kerosene-fuelled taxis were strictly a rich man's occa-
sional luxury—was bogged down almost at once in the
groaning, swaying crowd.

The main noise came from the big plastic proscenium,
where one of the lay preachers was exhorting the crowd
in a voice so heavily amplified as to be nearly unintel-
ligible. Witnesses with portable tape recorders, bags of
tracts and magazines, sandwich-boards lettered with
fluorescent inks, confessions for sinners to sign, and
green baize pokes for collections were well scattered

among the pedestrians, and the streets were crossed about every fifteen feet with the straight black snakes of compressed-air triggers.

As the Caddy pulled up for the second time, a nozzle was thrust into the rear window and a stream of iridescent bubbles poured across the back seat directly under Paige's and Anne's noses. As each bubble burst, there was a wave of perfume—evidently it was "Celestial Joy" the Witnesses were using this year—and a sweet voice said:

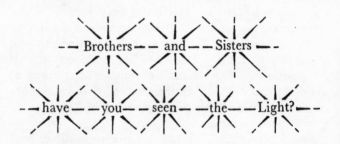

Paige fought at the bubbles with futile windmillings, while Anne Abbott leaned back against the cushions of the Caddy and watched him, with a faint smile of contemptuous amusement. The last bubble contained no word, but only an overpowering burst of odour. Despite herself, the girl's smile deepened: the perfume, in addition to being powerfully euphoric, was slightly aphrodisiac as well. This year, apparently, the Witnesses were readier than ever to use any means that came to hand.

The driver lurched the Caddy ahead. Then, before Paige could begin to grasp what was happening, the car stopped, the door next to the steering wheel was wrenched open, and four spidery, many-fingered arms plucked the driver neatly from his seat and deposited him on his knees on the asphalt outside.

"SHAME! SHAME!" the popai-robot thundered. "YOUR SINS HAVE FOUND YOU OUT! REPENT, AND FIND FORGIVENESS!"

A thin glass globe of some gas, evidently a narco-synthetic, broke beside the car, and not only the unfortunate chauffeur but also the part of the crowd which had begun to collect about him—mostly women, of course—began to weep convulsively.

"REPENT!" the robot intoned, over a sneaked-in choir now singing "Ah-ah-ah-ah-ah-h-h-h-h" somewhere in the warm evening air. "REPENT, FOR THE TIME IS AT HAND!"

Paige, astonished to find himself choking with sourceless, maudlin self-pity, flung himself out of the Caddy in search of a nose to break. But there were no live Witnesses in sight. The members of the order, all of whom were charged with spreading the good work by whatever means seemed good to them, had learned decades ago that their proselytizing was often resented, and had substituted technology for personal salesmanship wherever possible.

Their machines, too, had been forced to learn. The point-of-purchase robot retreated as Paige bore down upon it. The thing had been conditioned against allowing itself to be broken.

The Caddy's driver, rescued, blew his nose resentfully and started the car again. The wordless choir, with its eternal bridge-passage straight out of the compositions of Dmitri Tiomkin, diminished behind them, and the voice of the lay preacher came roaring back through to them over the fading, characterless music.

47

"I say to you," the p.a. system was moaning unctuously, like a lady hippopotamus reading A. E. Housman, "I say to you, the world and the things which are the world's come to an end and a quick end. In his overweening pride, man has sought even to wrest the stars from their courses, but the stars are not man's, and he shall rue that day. Ah, vanity of vanities, all is vanity (Preacher V: 796). Even on mighty Jove man dared to erect a great Bridge, as once in Babel he sought to build a tower to heaven. But this also is vanity, it is vicious pride and defiance, and it too shall bring calamity upon men. Pull down thy vanity, I say pull down! (Ezra lxxxi, 99.) Let there be an end to pride, and there shall be peace. Let there be love, and there shall be understanding. I say to you——"

At this point, the Witnesses' over-enthusiastic boobytrapping of the square cut off whatever the preacher was going to say next, as far as the occupants of the Caddy were concerned. The car passed over another trigger, and there was a blinding, rose-coloured flash. When Paige could see again, the car seemed to be floating in mid-air, and there were actual angels flapping solemnly around it. The *vox humana* of a Hammond organ sobbed among the clouds.

Paige supposed that the Witnesses had managed to crystallize temporarily, perhaps with a supersonic pulse, the glass of the windows, which he had rolled up to prevent another intromission of bubbles, and to project a 3-V tape against the glass crystals with polarized ultraviolet light. The random distribution of fluorescent trace compounds in ordinary window glass would account for the odd way the "angels" changed colour as they moved.

Understanding the vision's probable *modus operandi*

48

left Paige no less furious at the new delay, but luckily the thing turned out to be a trick left over from last year's Revival, for which the Caddy was prepared. The driver touched something on the dash and the saccharine scene vanished, hymns and all. The car lunged abruptly through an opening in the crowd, and a moment later the square was behind them.

"Whew!" Paige said, leaning back at last. "Now I understand why taxi depots have vending machines for trip-insurance policies. The Witnesses weren't much in evidence the last time I was on Earth."

"Every tenth person you meet is a Witness now," Anne said. "And eight of the other nine claim that they've given up religion as a bad job. While you're caught in the middle of one of those Revivals, though, it's hard to believe the complaints you read about our times—that people have no faith and so on."

"I don't find it so," Paige said reflectively. This certainly did not strike him as light social conversation, but since it was instead a kind of talk he much more enjoyed—talk which was about something—he could only be delighted that the ice was broken. "I've no religion of my own, but I think that when the experts talk about 'faith' they mean something different than the shouting kind, the kind the Witnesses have. Shouting religions always strike me as essentially like pep-meetings among salesmen; their ceremonies and their manners are so aggressive because they don't really believe the code themselves. Real faith is so much a part of the world you live in that you seldom notice it, and it isn't always religious in the formal sense. Mathematics is based on faith, for instance, for those who know it."

"I should have said that it was based on the antithesis of faith," Anne said, turning a little cooler. "Have you had any experience in the field, Colonel?"

"Some," he said, without rancour. "I'd never have been allowed to pilot a ship outside the orbit of the Moon without knowing tensors, and if I expect to get my next promotion, I'm going to have to know spinor calculus as well—which I do."

"Oh," the girl said. She sounded faintly dashed. "Go on; I'm sorry I interrupted."

"You were right to interrupt; I made my point badly. I meant to say that the mathematician's belief that there is some relationship between maths and the real world is a faith; it can't be proven, but he feels it very strongly. For that matter, the totally irreligious man's belief that there even *is* a real world, corresponding to what his senses show him, can't be proven. John Doe and the most brilliant of physicists both have to take that on faith."

"And they don't conduct ceremonies symbolizing the belief," Anne added, "and train specialists to reassure them of it every seven days."

"That's right. In the same way, John Doe used to feel that the basic religions of the West had some relationship to the real world which was valid, even though it couldn't be proven. And that includes Communism, which was born in the West, after all. John Doe doesn't feel that way any more—and by my guess, neither do the Witnesses, or they wouldn't be shouting so loud. In that sense, there's not much faith lying around loose these days anywhere, as far as I can see. None for me to pick up, that much I've found out the hard way."

"Har y'are," the chauffeur said.

Paige helped the girl out of the car, trying not to notice how much fare he had to pay, and the two were shown to a table in the restaurant. Anne was silent again for a while after they were seated. Paige had about decided that she had chosen to freeze up once more, and had begun to wonder if he could arrange to have the place invaded by Witnesses to start the conversation again, when she said:

"You seem to have been thinking about faith quite a bit. You talk as though the problem meant something to you. Could you tell me why?"

"I'd be glad to try," he said slowly. "The standard answer would be that while you're out in space you have lots of time to think—but people use thinking-time differently. I suppose I've been looking for some frame of reference that could be mine ever since I was four, when my father and mother split up. She was a Christian Scientist and he was a Dianeticist, so they had a lot to fight about. There was a court battle over custody that lasted for nearly five years.

"I joined the Army when I was seventeen, and it didn't take me very long to find out that the Army is no substitute for a family, let alone a church. Then I volunteered for space service school. That was no church either. The Army got jurisdiction over space travel when the whole field was just a baby, because it had a long tradition of grafting off land-grants, and it didn't want the Navy or the Air Force to grab off the gravy from any such grants that might be made on the planets. I spent more time helping the Army space-travel department fight unification with the space arms of the other services than I did doing real work in space. That was what I was ordered to do—but it didn't help me to think of space as the ultimate cathedral. . . .

"Somewhere along in there, I got married and we had one son; he was born the same day I entered space school.

51

Two years later, the marriage was annulled. That sounds funny, I know, but the circumstances were unusual.

"When Pfitzner approached me and asked me to pick up soil samples for them, I suppose I saw another church with which I could identify myself—something humanitarian, long-range, impersonal. And when I found this afternoon that the new church wasn't going to welcome the convert with glad cries—well, the result is that I'm now weeping on your shoulder." He smiled. "That's hardly flattering, I know. But you've already helped me to talk myself into a spot where the only next step is to apologize, which I hereby do. I hope you'll accept it."

"I think I will," she said, and then, tentatively, she smiled back. The result made him tingle as though the air-pressure had dropped suddenly by five pounds per square inch. Anne Abbott was one of those exceedingly rare plain girls whose smiles completely transform them, as abruptly as the bursting of a star-shell. When she wore her normal, rather sullen expression, no one would ever notice her—but a man who had seen her smile might well be willing to kill himself working to make her smile again, as often as possible. A woman who was beautiful all the time, Paige thought, probably never could know the devotion Anne Abbott would be given, when she found that man.

"Thank you," Paige said, rather inadequately. "Let's order, and then I'd like to hear you talk. I dumped the Story of My Life into your lap rather early in the game, I'm afraid."

"You order," she said. "You talked about seafood this afternoon, so you must know the menu here—and you handed me out of the Caddy so nicely that I'd like to preserve the illusion."

"Illusion?"

"Don't make me explain," she said, colouring faintly. "But. . . . Well, the illusion of there being one or two cavaliers in the world still. Since you haven't been a surplus woman on a planet full of lazy males, you wouldn't understand the value of a small courtesy or two. Most men I meet want to be shown my garters before they'll bother to learn my last name."

Paige's surprised shout of laughter made heads turn all over the restaurant. He throttled it hurriedly, afraid that it would embarrass the girl, but she was smiling again, making him feel instead as though he had just had three whiskies in quick succession.

"That's a quick transformation for me," he said. "This afternoon I was a blackmailer, and by my own intention, too. Very well, then, let's have the flounder; it's a speciality of the house. I had visions of it, while I was on Ganymede munching my concentrates."

"I think you had the right idea about Pfitzner," Anne said slowly when the waiter had gone. "I can't tell you any secrets about it, but maybe I can tell you some bits of common knowledge that you evidently don't know. The project the plant is working on now seems to me to fit your description exactly: it's humanitarian, impersonal, and just about as long-range as any project I can imagine. I feel rather religious about it, in your sense. It's something to tie to, and it's better for me than being a Witness or a WAC. And I think you could understand why I feel that way—better than either Tru Gunn or I thought you could."

It was his turn to be embarrassed. He covered by dosing his Blue Points with Worcestershire until they flinched visibly. "I'd like to know."

"It goes like this," she said. "In between 1940 and

1960, a big change took place in Western medicine. Before 1940—in the early part of the century—the infectious diseases were major killers. By 1960 they were all but knocked out of the running. The change started with the sulfa drugs; then came Fleming and Florey and mass production of penicillin during World War II. After that war we found a whole arsenal of new drugs against tuberculosis, which had really never been treated successfully before—streptomycin, PAS, isoniazid, viomycin, and so on, right up to Bloch's isolation of the TB toxins and the development of the metabolic blocking agents.

"Then came the broad-spectrum antibiotics, like terramycin, which attacked some virus diseases, protozoan diseases, even worm diseases; that gave us a huge clue to a whole set of tough problems. The last major infectious disease—bilharzia, or schistosomiasis—was reduced to the status of a nuisance by 1966."

"But we still have infectious diseases," Paige objected.

"Of course we do," the girl said, the little atompoints in her brooch picking up the candle-light as she leaned forward. "No drug ever wipes out a disease, because it's impossible to kill all the dangerous organisms in the world just by treating the patients they invade. But you can reduce the danger. In the 1950s, for instance, malaria was the world's greatest killer. Now it's as rare as diphtheria. We still have both diseases with us—but how long has it been since you heard of a case of either?"

"You're asking the wrong man—germ diseases aren't common on space vessels. But you win the point, all the same. Go on. What happened then?"

"Something kind of ominous. Life insurance companies, and other people who kept records, began to be

54

alarmed at the way the degenerative diseases were coming to the fore. Those are such ailments as hardening of the arteries, coronary heart disease, embolisms, and almost all the many forms of cancer—diseases where one or another body mechanism suddenly goes haywire, without any visible cause."

"Isn't old age the cause?"

"*No,*" the girl said forcefully. "Old age is just the *age*; it's not a thing in itself, it's just the time of life when most degenerative diseases strike. Some of them prefer children—leukemia, for instance. When the actuaries first began to notice that the degenerative diseases were on the rise, they thought that it was just a sort of side-effect of the decline of the infectious diseases. They thought that cancer was increasing because more people were living long enough to come down with it. Also, the reporting of the degenerative diseases was improving, and so part of the rise in incidence really was an illusion—it just meant that more cases than before were being detected.

"But that wasn't all there was to it. Lung cancer and stomach cancer in particular continued to creep up the statistical tables, far beyond the point which could have been accounted for by better reporting, or by the increase in the average life-span, either. Then the same thing took place in malignant hypertension, in Parkinsonism and other failures of the central nervous system, in muscular dystrophy, and so on, and so on. It began to look very much as though we'd exchanged a devil we knew for a devil we didn't.

"So there was quite a long search for a possible infectious origin for each of the degenerative diseases. Because some animal tumours, like poultry sarcoma, are caused by viruses, a lot of people set to work hunt-

55

ing like mad for all kinds of cancer viruses. There was a concerted attempt to implicate a group called the pleuropneumonia-like organisms as the cause of the arthritic diseases. The vascular diseases, like hypertension and thrombosis, got blamed on everything from your diet to your grandmother.

"And it all came to very little. Oh, we did find that *some* viruses did cause *some* types of cancer, leukemia among them. The PPLO group does cause *a* type of arthritis, too, but only the type associated with a venereal disease called essential urethritis. And we found that the commonest of the three types of lung cancer was being caused by the radio-potassium content of tobacco smoke; it was the lip and mouth cancers that were caused by the tars. But for the most part, we found out just what we had known before—that the degenerative diseases weren't infectious. We'd already been down *that* dead end.

"About there was when Pfitzner got into the picture. The NHS, the National Health Service, got alarmed enough about the rising incidence-curves to call the first really major world congress on the degenerative diseases. The U.S. paid part of the bill because the armed services were getting nervous about the rising rate of draft rejections they were being forced to return. It doesn't seem unusual now that 10 per cent of a given class of men in their twenties should be rejected for what we still call 'diseases of old age', but in those days it was shocking."

"It shocks me right now," Paige admitted.

"Only because it's new to you, I'm afraid. It's old stuff to the armed services' medical departments now. Anyhow, the result of the congress was that the U.S. Department of Health, Welfare and Security somehow

56

got a billion-dollar appropriation for a real mass attack on the degenerative diseases. In case you drop zeros as easily as I do, that was about half what had been spent to produce the first atomic bomb. Since then, the appropriation has been added to once, and it's due for renewal again now.

"Pfitzner holds the major contract on that project, and we're well enough staffed and equipped to handle it so that we've had to do very little sub-contracting. We simply share the appropriation with three other producers of biologicals, two of whom are producers only and so have no hand in the research; the third firm has done as much research as we have, but we know—because this is supposed to be a co-ordinated effort with sharing of knowledge among the contractors—that they're far gone down another blind alley. We would have told them so, but after one look at what *we'd* found, the government decided that the fewer people who knew about it, the better. We didn't mind; after all, we're in business to make a profit, too. But that's one reason why you saw so many government people on our necks this afternoon."

The girl broke off abruptly and delved into her pocket-book, producing a flat compact which she opened and inspected intently. Since she wore almost no make-up, it was hard to imagine the reason for the sudden examination; but after a brief, odd smile at one corner of her mouth, she tucked the compact away again.

"The other reason," she said "is even simpler, now that you have the background. *We've just found what we think may be a major key to the whole problem.*"

"Wow," Paige said, inelegantly but *affetuoso*.

"Or zowie, or biff-bam-krunk," Anne agreed calmly,

57

"or maybe God-help-us-every-one. But so far the thing's held up. It's passed every test. If it keeps up that performance, Pfitzner will get the whole of the new appropriation—and if it doesn't, there may not be any appropriation at all, not only for Pfitzner, but for the other firms that have been helping on the project.

"The whole question of whether or not we lick the degenerative diseases hangs on those two things: the validity of the solution we've found, and the money. If one goes, the other goes. And we'll have to tell Horsefield and MacHinery and the others what we've found some time this month, because the old appropriation lapses after that."

The girl leaned back and seemed to notice for the first time that she had finished her dinner. "And that," she said, pushing regretfully at the sprig of parsley with her fork, "isn't exactly public knowledge yet! I think I'd better shut up."

"Thank you," Paige said gravely. "It's obviously more than I deserve to know."

"Well," Anne said, "you can tell *me* something, if you will. It's about this Bridge that's being built on Jupiter. Is it worth all the money that they're pouring into it? Nobody seems to be able to explain what it's good for. And now there's talk that another Bridge'll be started on Saturn, when this one's finished!"

"You needn't worry," Paige said. "Understand, I've no connection with the Bridge, though I do know some people on the Bridge gang, so I haven't any inside information. I do have some public knowledge, just like yours—meaning knowledge that anyone can have, if he has the training to know where to look for it. As I understand it, the Bridge on Jupiter is a research project, designed to answer some questions—just what questions, nobody's bothered to tell me, and I've been careful not to ask; you can see Francis X. MacHinery's face in the constellations if you look carefully enough. But this much I know: the conditions of the research demand the use of the largest planet in the system. That's Jupiter, so it would be senseless to build another Bridge on a smaller planet, like Saturn. The Bridge gang will keep the present structure going until they've found out what they want to know. Then the project will almost surely be discontinued—not because the Bridge is 'finished', but because it will have served its purpose."

"I suppose I'm showing my ignorance," Anne said, "but it sounds idiotic to me. All those millions and millions of dollars—that *we* could be saving lives with!"

"If the choice were mine," Paige agreed, "I'd award the money to you, not to Charity Dillon and his crew. But then, I know almost as little about the Bridge as you do, so perhaps it's just as well that I'm not allowed to route the check. Is it my turn to ask a question? I still have a small one."

"Your witness," Anne said, smiling her altogether lovely smile.

"This afternoon, while I was in the labs, I twice heard a baby crying—and I think it was actually two different babies. I asked your Mr. Gunn about it, and he told me an obvious fairy-story." He paused. Anne's eyes had already begun to glitter.

"You're on dangerous ground, Colonel Russell," she said.

"I can tell. But I mean to ask my question anyhow. When I pulled my absurd vivisection threat on you later, I was out-and-out flabbergasted that it worked, but it set me to thinking. Can you explain—and if so, would you?"

59

Anne got out her compact again and seemed to consult it, warily. At last she said: "I suppose I've forgiven you, more or less. Anyhow, I'll answer. It's very simple: the babies *are* being used as experimental animals. We have a pipeline to the local foundling home. It's all only technically legal, and had you actually brought charges of human vivisection against us, you probably could have made them stick."

His coffee cup clattered into its saucer. "Great God, Anne. Isn't it dangerous to make such a joke these days —especially with a man you've known only half a day? Or are you trying to startle me into admitting I'm a stoolie?"

"I'm not joking and I don't think you're a stoolie," she said calmly. "What I said was perfectly true—oh, I souped up the way I put it just a little, maybe because I haven't *entirely* forgiven you for that bit of successful blackmail, and I wanted to see you jump. And for other reasons. But it's true."

"But Anne—why?"

"Look, Paige," she said. "It was fifty years ago that we found that if we added minute amounts of certain antibiotics, really just traces, to animal feeds, the addition brought the critters to market months ahead of normally-fed animals. For that matter, it even provokes growth spurts in plants under special conditions; and it works for poultry, piglets, calves, mink cubs, a whole spectrum of animals. It was logical to suspect that it might work in newborn humans, too."

"And you're trying that?" Paige leaned back and poured himself another glass of Chilean Rhine. "I'd say you souped up your revelation quite a bit, all right."

"Don't be so ready to accept the obvious, and listen to me. We are *not* doing that. It was done decades ago,

60

regularly and above the board, by students of Paul György and half a hundred other nutrition experts. Those people used only very widely known and tested antibiotics, drugs that had already been used on literally millions of farm animals, dosages worked out to the milligram of drug per kilogram of body weight, and so on. But this particular growth-stimulating effect of antibiotics happens to be a major clue to whether or not a given drug has the kind of biological activity *we* want— and we have to know whether or not it shows that activity *in human beings*. So we screen new drugs on the kids, as fast as they're found and pass certain other tests. We have to."

"I see," Paige said. "I see."

"The children are 'volunteered' by the foundling home, and we could make a show of legality if it came to a court fight," Anne said. "The precedent was established in 1952, when Pearl River Labs used children of its own workers to test its polio vaccine—which worked, by the way. But it isn't the legality of it that's important. It's the question of how soon and how thoroughly we're going to lick the degenerative diseases."

"You seem to be defending it to me," Paige said slowly, "as though you cared what I thought about it. So I'll tell you what I think: it seems mighty damned cold-blooded to me. It's the kind of thing of which ugly myths are made. If ten years from now there's a pogrom against biologists because people think they eat babies, I'll know why."

"Nonsense," Anne said. "It takes centuries to build up that kind of myth. You're over-reacting."

"On the contrary. I'm being as honest with you as you were with me. I'm astonished and somewhat repelled by what you've told me. That's all."

61

The girl, her lips slightly thinned, dipped and dried her fingertips and began to draw on her gloves. "Then we'll say no more about it," she said. "I think we'd better leave now."

"Certainly, as soon as I pay the check. Which reminds me: do you have any interest in Pfitzner, Anne—a personal interest, I mean?"

"No. No more interest than any human being with a moment's understanding of the implications would have. And I think that's a rather ugly sort of question."

"I thought you might take it that way, but I really wasn't accusing you of being a profiteer. I just wondered whether or not you were related to the Dr. Abbott that Gunn and the rest were waiting for this afternoon."

She got out the compact again and looked carefully into it. "Abbott's a common enough name."

"Sure. Still, *some* Abbotts are related. And it seems to make sense."

"Let's hear you do that. I'd be interested."

"All right," he said, beginning to become angry himself. "The receptionist at Pfitzner, ideally, should know exactly what is going on in the plant at all times, so as to be able to assess accurately the intentions of every visitor—just as you did with me. But at the same time, she has to be an absolutely flawless security risk, or otherwise she couldn't be trusted with enough knowledge to be that kind of a receptionist. The best way to make sure of the security angle is to hire someone with a blood tie to another person on the project. That adds up to *two* people who are being careful. A classical Soviet form of blackmail, as I recall.

"That much is theory. There's fact, too. You certainly explained the Pfitzner project to me this evening from a broad base of knowledge that nobody could expect to find in an ordinary receptionist. On top of that, you took policy risks that, properly, only an officer of Pfitzner should be empowered to take. I conclude that you're not *only* a receptionist; your name is Abbott; and . . . there we have it, it seems to me."

"Do we?" the girl said, standing abruptly in a white fury. "Not quite! Also, I'm not pretty, and a receptionist for a firm as big as Pfitzner is usually pretty striking. Striking enough to resist being pumped by the first man to notice her, at least. Go ahead, complete the list! Tell the whole truth!"

"How can I?" Paige said, rising also and looking squarely at her, his fingers closing slowly. "If I told you honestly just what I think of your looks—and by God I will, I think the most beautiful woman in the world would bathe every day in fuming nitric acid just to duplicate your smile—you'd hate me more than ever. You'd think I was mocking you. Now you tell me the rest of the truth. You *are* related to Dr. Abbott."

"Patly enough," the girl said, each word cut out of smoking-dry ice, "Dr. Abbott is my father. And I insist upon being allowed to go home now, Colonel Russell. Not ten seconds from now, but *now*."

4

The Bridge vanished. Helmuth set the heavy helmet carefully in its niche and felt of his temples, feeling the blood passing under his fingertips. Then he turned.

Dillon was looking at him.

"Well?" the civil engineer said. "What's the matter, Bob? Is it bad——?"

Helmuth did not reply for a moment. The abrupt transition from the storm-ravaged deck of the Bridge to the quiet, placid air of the operations shack on Jupiter's fifth moon was always a shock. He had never been able to anticipate it, let alone become accustomed to it; it was worse each time, not better.

He pulled the jacks from the foreman's board and let them flick back into the desk on their alive, elastic cables, and then got up from the bucket seat, moving carefully upon shaky legs, feeling implicit in his own body the enormous weights and pressures his guiding intelligence had just quitted. The fact that the gravity on the foreman's deck was as weak as that of most of the habitable asteroids only made the contrast greater, and his need for caution in walking more extreme.

He went to the big porthole and looked out. The unworn, tumbled, monotonous surface of airless Jupiter V looked almost homey after the perpetual holocaust of Jupiter itself. But there was an overpowering reminder

64

of that holocaust—for through the thick quartz of the porthole, the face of the giant planet stared at Helmuth, across only 112,600 miles, less than half the distance between Earth's moon and Earth; a sphere-section occupying almost all of the sky, except the near horizon, where one could see a few first-magnitude stars. The rest of the sky was crawling with colour, striped and blotched with the eternal, frigid, poisonous storming of Jupiter's atmosphere, spotted with the deep-black, planet-sized shadows of moons closer to the sun than Jupiter V.

Somewhere down there, six thousand miles below the clouds that boiled in Helmuth's face, was the Bridge. The Bridge was thirty miles high and eleven miles wide and fifty-four miles long—but it was only a sliver, an intricate and fragile arrangement of ice-crystals beneath the bulging, racing tornadoes.

On Earth, even in the West, the Bridge would have been the mightiest engineering achievement of all history, could the Earth have borne its weight at all. But on Jupiter, the Bridge was as precarious and perishable as a snowflake.

"Bob?" Dillon's voice asked. "What is it? You seem more upset than usual. Is it serious?"

Helmuth looked up. His superior's worn young face, lantern-jawed and crowned by black hair already beginning to grey at the temples, was alight both with love for the Bridge and with the consuming ardour of the responsibility he had to bear. As always, it touched Helmuth, and reminded him that the implacable universe had, after all, provided one warm corner in which human beings might huddle together.

"Serious enough," he said, forming the words with difficulty against the frozen inarticulateness Jupiter had forced upon him. "But not fatal, as far as I could see. There's a lot of hydrogen vulcanism on the surface, especially at the north-west end, and it looks like there must have been a big blast under the cliffs. I saw what looked like the last of a series of fire-falls."

Dillon's face relaxed while Helmuth was talking, slowly, line by engraved line. "Oh. It was just a flying chunk, then."

"I'm almost sure that was what it was. The cross-draughts are heavy now. The Spot and the STD are due to pass each other some time next month, aren't they? I haven't checked, but I can feel the difference in the storms."

"So the chunk got picked up and thrown through the end of the Bridge. A big piece?"

Helmuth shrugged. "That end is all twisted away to the left, and the deck is burst into matchwood. The scaffolding is all gone, too, of course. A pretty big piece, all right, Charity—two miles through at a minimum."

Dillon sighed. He, too, went to the window, and looked out. Helmuth did not need to be a mind reader to know what he was looking at. Out there, across the stony waste of Jupiter V plus 112,600 miles of space, the South Tropical Disturbance was streaming toward the Great Red Spot, and would soon overtake it. When the whirling funnel of the STD—more than big enough to suck three Earths into deep-freeze—passed the planetary island of sodium-tainted ice which was the Red Spot, the Spot would follow it for a few thousand miles, at the same time rising closer to the surface of the atmosphere.

Then the Spot would sink again, drifting back toward the incredible jet of stress-fluid which kept it in being— a jet fed by no one knew what forces at Jupiter's hot, rocky, 22,000-mile core, compacted down there under

16,000 miles of eternal ice. During the entire passage, the storms all over Jupiter became especially violent; and the Bridge had been forced to locate in anything but the calmest spot on the planet, thanks to the uneven distribution of the few "permanent" land-masses.

But—"permanent"? The quote-marks Helmuth's thinking always put around that word were there for a very good reason, he knew, but he could not quite remember the reason. It was the damned conditioning showing itself again, creating another of the thousand small irreconcilables which contributed to the tension.

Helmuth watched Dillon with a certain compassion, tempered with mild envy. Charity Dillon's unfortunate given name betrayed him as the son of a hangover, the only male child of a Witness family which dated back long before the current resurgence of the Witnesses. He was one of the hundreds of government-drafted experts who had planned the Bridge, and he was as obsessed by the Bridge as Helmuth was—but for different reasons. It was widely believed among the Bridge gang that Dillon, alone among them, had not been given the conditioning, but there was no way to test that.

Helmuth moved back to the port, dropping his hand gently on Dillon's shoulder. Together they looked at the screaming straw yellows, brick reds, pinks, oranges, browns, even blues and greens that Jupiter threw across the ruined stone of its innermost satellite. On Jupiter V, even the shadows had colour.

Dillon did not move. He said at last: "Are you pleased, Bob?"

"Pleased?" Helmuth said in astonishment. "No. It scares me white; you know that. I'm just glad that the whole Bridge didn't go."

"You're quite sure?" Dillon said quietly.

Helmuth took his hand from Dillon's shoulder and returned to his seat at the central desk. "You've no right to needle me for something I can't help," he said, his voice even lower than Dillon's. "I work on Jupiter four hours a day—not actually, because we can't keep a man alive for more than a split second down there—but my eyes and my ears and my mind are there, on the Bridge, four hours a day. Jupiter is not a nice place. I don't like it. I won't pretend I do.

"Spending four hours a day in an environment like that over a period of years—well, the human mind instinctively tries to adapt, even to the unthinkable. Sometimes I wonder how I'll behave when I'm put back in Chicago again. Sometimes I can't remember anything about Chicago except vague generalities, sometimes I can't even believe there is such a place as Earth —how could there be, when the rest of the universe is like Jupiter, or worse?"

"I know," Dillon said. "I've tried several times to show you that isn't a very reasonable frame of mind."

"I know it isn't. But I can't help how I feel. For all I know it isn't even my own frame of mind—though the part of my mind that keeps saying 'The Bridge *must* stand' is more likely to be the conditioned part. No, I don't think the Bridge will last. It can't last; it's all wrong. But I don't *want* to see it go. I've just got sense enough to know that one of these days Jupiter is going to sweep it away."

He wiped an open palm across the control boards, snapping all the toggles to "Off" with a sound like the fall of a double-handful of marbles on a pane of glass. "Like that, Charity! And I work four hours a day, every day, on the Bridge. One of these days, Jupiter is going to destroy the Bridge. It'll go flying away in little flinders, into the storms. My mind will be there, supervising some puny job, and my mind will go flying away along with my mechanical eyes and ears and hands—still trying to adapt to the unthinkable, tumbling away into the winds and the flames and the rains and the darkness and the pressure and the cold——"

"Bob, you're deliberately running away with yourself. Cut it out. Cut it out, I say!"

Helmuth shrugged, putting a trembling hand on the edge of the board to steady himself. "All right. I'm all right, Charity. I'm here, aren't I? Right here on Jupiter V, in no danger, in no danger at all. The Bridge is one hundred and twelve thousand six hundred miles away from here, and I'll never be an inch closer to it. But when the day comes that the Bridge is swept away——"

"Charity, sometimes I imagine you ferrying my body back to the cosy nook it came from, while my soul goes tumbling and tumbling through millions of cubic miles of poison. . . . All right, Charity, I'll be good. I won't think about it out loud, but you can't expect me to forget it. It's on my mind; I can't help it, and you should know that."

"I do," Dillon said, with a kind of eagerness. "I do, Bob. I'm only trying to help, to make you see the problem as it is. The Bridge isn't really that awful, it isn't worth a single nightmare."

"Oh, it isn't the Bridge that makes me yell out when I'm sleeping," Helmuth said, smiling bitterly. "I'm not that ridden by it yet. It's while I'm awake that I'm afraid the Bridge will be swept away. What I sleep with is a fear of myself."

"That's a sane fear. You're as sane as any of us," Dillon insisted, fiercely solemn. "Look, Bob. The Bridge isn't a monster. It's a way we've developed for studying the behaviour of materials under specific conditions of pressure, temperature and gravity. Jupiter isn't Hell, either; it's a set of conditions. The Bridge is the laboratory we set up to work with those conditions."

"It isn't going anywhere. It's a bridge to noplace."

"There aren't many *places* on Jupiter," Dillon said, missing Helmuth's meaning entirely. "We put the Bridge on an island in the local sea because we needed solid ice we could sink the foundation in. Otherwise, it wouldn't have mattered where we put it. We could have floated the caissons on the sea itself, if we hadn't wanted a fixed point from which to measure storm velocities and such things."

"I know that," Helmuth said.

"But Bob, you don't show any signs of understanding it. Why, for instance, should the Bridge *go* any place? It isn't even, properly speaking, a bridge at all. We only call it that because we used some bridge engineering principles in building it. Actually, it's much more like a travelling crane—an extremely heavy-duty overhead rail line. It isn't going anywhere because it hasn't any place interesting to go to, that's all. We're extending it to cover as much territory as possible, and to increase its stability, not to span the distance between places. There's no point to reproaching it because it doesn't span a real gap—between, say, Dover and Calais. It's a bridge to knowledge, and that's far more important. Why can't you see that?"

"I can see that; that's what I was talking about," Helmuth said, trying to control his impatience. "I have at least as much common sense as the average child. What I was trying to point out is that meeting colossalness with colossalness—out here—is a mug's game. It's a game Jupiter will always win, without the

70

slightest effort. What if the engineers who built the Dover-Calais bridge had been limited to broom-straws for their structural members? They could have got the bridge up somehow, sure, and made it strong enough to carry light traffic on a fair day. But what would you have had left of it after the first winter storm came down the Channel from the North Sea? The whole approach is idiotic!"

"All right," Dillon said reasonably. "You have a point. Now you're being reasonable. What better approach have you to suggest? Should we abandon Jupiter entirely because it's too big for us?"

"No," Helmuth said. "Or maybe, yes. I don't know. I don't have any easy answer. I just know that this one is no answer at all—it's just a cumbersome evasion."

Dillon smiled. "You're depressed, and no wonder. Sleep it off, Bob, if you can—you might even come up with that answer. In the meantime—well, when you stop to think about it, the surface of Jupiter isn't any more hostile, inherently, than the surface of Jupiter V, except in degree. If you stepped out of this building naked, you'd die just as fast as you would on Jupiter. Try to look at it that way."

Helmuth, looking forward into another night of dreams, said: "That's the way I look at it now."

BOOK TWO

INTERMEZZO

The report of the investigating sub-committee of the Senate Finance Committee on the Jupiter Project was a massive document, especially so in the mimeographed, uncorrected form in which it had been rushed to Wagoner's desk. In its printed form—not due for another two weeks—the report would be considerably less bulky, but it would probably be more unreadable. In addition, it would be tempered in spots by the cautious second thoughts of its seven authors; Wagoner needed to see their opinions in the raw or "for colleagues only" version.

Not that the printed version would get a much wider circulation. Even the mimeographed document was stamped "Top Secret". It had been years since anything about the government's security system had amused Wagoner in the slightest, but he could not repress a wry grin now. Of course the Bridge itself was Top Secret; but had the sub-committee's report been ready only a little over a year ago, everybody in the country would have heard about it, and selected passages would have been printed in the newspapers. He could think offhand of at least ten opposition senators, and two or three more inside his own party, who had been determined to use the report to prevent his re-election—or any parts of the report that might have been turned to that purpose. Unhappily for them, the report had been still only a third finished when election day had come, and Alaska had sent Wagoner back to Washington by a very comfortable plurality.

And, as he turned the stiff legal-length pages slowly, with the pleasant smoky odour of duplicator ink rising from them as he turned, it became clear that the report would have made pretty poor campaign material anyhow. Much of it was highly technical, and had obviously been written by staff advisers, not by the investigating senators themselves. The public might be impressed by, but it could not read and would not read, such a show of erudition. Besides, it was only a show; nearly all the technical discussions of the Bridge's problems petered out into meaningless generalities. In most such instances Wagoner was able to put a mental finger on the missing fact, the ignorance or the withholding of which had left the chain of reasoning suspended in mid-air.

Against the actual operation of the Bridge the senators had been able to find nothing of substance to say. Given in advance the fact that the taxpayers had wanted to spend so much money to build a Bridge on Jupiter—which is to say, somebody (Wagoner himself) had decided that for them, without confusing them by bringing the proposition to their attention—then even the opposition senators had had to agree that it had been built as economically as possible, and was still being built that way.

Of course, there had been small grafts waiting to be discovered, and the investigators had discovered them. One of the supply-ship captains had been selling cakes of soap to the crew on Ganymede at incredible prices, with the co-operation of the stores clerk there. But that

was nothing more than a book-keeper's crime, on a project the size of the Bridge. Wagoner a little admired the supply-ship captain's ingenuity—or had it been the stores clerk's?—in discovering an item wanted badly enough on Ganymede, and small enough, and light enough, to be worth smuggling. The men on the Bridge gang banked most of their salaries automatically on Earth without ever seeing them; there was very little worth buying, or selling, on the moons of Jupiter.

Of major graft, however, there had been no trace. No steel company had sold the Bridge any sub-standard castings, because there was no steel in the Bridge. A Jovian might have made a good thing of selling the Bridge sub-standard Ice IV—but as far as anyone could know there were no Jovians, so the Bridge got its Ice IV for nothing but the cost of cutting it. Wagoner's office had been very strict about the handling of the lesser contracts—for prefabricated moon huts, for supply ferry fuel, for equipment—and had policed not only its own deals, but all the Army Space Service sub-contracts connected with the Bridge.

As for Charity Dillon and his foremen, they were rigidly efficient—partly because it was in their natures to work that way, and partly because of the intensive conditioning they had all been given before being shipped to the Jovian system. There was no waste to be found in anything that they supervised, and if they had occasionally been guilty of bad engineering judgment, no outside engineer would be likely to detect it. The engineering principles by which the Bridge operated did not hold true anywhere but on Jupiter.

The hugest loss of money the whole Jupiter Project had yet sustained had been accompanied by such carnage that it fell—in the senators' minds—in the category of warfare. When a soldier is killed by enemy action, nobody asks how much money his death cost the government through the loss of his gear. The part of the report which described the placing of the Bridge's foundation mentioned reverently the heroism of the lost two hundred and thirty-one crewmen; it said nothing about the cost of the nine specially-designed space tugs which now floated in silhouette, as flat as so many tin cut-outs under six million pounds per square inch of pressure, somewhere at the bottom of Jupiter's atmosphere—floated with eight thousand vertical miles of eternally roaring poisons between them and the eyes of the living.

Had those crewmen been heroes? They had been enlisted men and officers of the Army Space Service, acting under orders. While doing what they had been ordered to do, they had been killed. Wagoner could not remember whether or not the survivors of that operation had also been called heroes. Oh, they had certainly been decorated—the Army liked its men to wear as much fruit salad on their chests as it could possibly spoon out to them, because it was good public relations—but they were not mentioned in the report.

This much was certain: the dead men had died because of Wagoner. He had known, generally at least, that many of them would die, but he had gone ahead anyhow. He knew now that there might be worse to come. Nevertheless, he would proceed, because he thought that—in the long run—it would be worth it. He knew well enough that the end cannot justify the means; but if there are *no* other means, and the end is necessary. . . .

But from time to time he thought of Dostoievski, and the Grand Inquisitor. Would the Millennium be worth having, if it could be ushered in only by the torturing

to death of a single child? What Wagoner foresaw and planned for was by no means the Millennium; and while the children at Jno. Pfitzner & Sons were certainly not being tortured or even harmed, their experiences there were at least not normal for children. And there were two hundred and thirty-one men frozen solid somewhere in the bottomless hell of Jupiter, men who had had to obey their orders even more helplessly than children.

Wagoner had not been cut out to be a general.

The report praised the lost men's heroism. Wagoner lifted the heavy pages one after another, looking for a word from the investigating senators about the cause those deaths had served. There was nothing there—nothing but the conventional phrases, "for their country", "for the cause of peace", "for the future". High-order abstractions—blabs. The senators had no notion of what the Bridge was for. They had looked, but they hadn't seen. Even with a total of four years to think back on the experience, they hadn't seen. The very size of the Bridge evidently had convinced them that it was a form of weapons research—so much for "for the cause of peace"—and that it would be better for them not to know the nature of the weapon until an official announcement was circulated to them.

They were right. The Bridge was assuredly a weapon. But in neglecting to wonder what kind of a weapon it might be, the senators had also neglected to wonder at whom it was pointed. Wagoner was glad that they had.

The report did not even touch upon those two years of exploration, of search for some project which might be worth attacking, which had preceded even the notion of the Bridge. Wagoner had had a special staff of four devoted men at work during every minute of those

79

two years, checking patents that had been granted but not sequestered, published scientific papers containing suggestions other scientists had decided not to explore, articles in the lay press about incipient miracles which hadn't come off, science-fiction stories by practising scientists, anything and everything that might lead somewhere. The four men had worked under orders to avoid telling anybody what they were looking for, and to stay strictly away from the main currents of modern scientific thought on the subject; but no secret is ever truly safe; no fact in nature is ever truly a secret.

Somewhere, for instance, in the files of the FBI, was a tape recording of the conversation he had had with the chief of the four-man team, in his office, the day the break came. The man had said, not only to Wagoner, but to the attentive FBI microphones no senator dared to seek out and muffle: "This looks like a real line, Bliss. On Subject G." (Something on gravity, chief.)

"Keep it to the point." (A reminder: Keep it too technical to interest a casual eavesdropper—if you *have* to talk about it here, with all these bugs to pick it up.)

"Sure. It's a thing called the Blackett equation. Deals with a possible relationship between electron-spin and magnetic moment. I understand Dirac did some work on that, too. There's a G in the equation, and with one simple algebraic manipulation you can isolate the G on one side of the equals-sign, and all the other elements on the other." (Not a crackpot notion this time. Real scientists have been interested in it. There's math to go with it.)

"Status?" (Why was it never followed, then?)

"The original equation is about status seven, but there's no way anybody knows that it could be subjected to an operational test. The manipulated equation

80

is called the Locke Derivation, and our boys say that a little dimensional analysis will show that it's wrong; but they're not entirely sure. However, it *is* subject to an operational test if we want to pay for it, where the original Blackett formula isn't." (Nobody's sure what it means yet. It may mean nothing. It would cost a hell of a lot to find out.)

"Do we have the facilities?" (Just how much?)

"Only the beginnings." (About four billion dollars, Bliss.)

"Conservatively?" (Why so much?)

"Yes. Field strength again."

(That was shorthand for the only problem that mattered, in the long run, if you wanted to work with gravity. Whether you thought of it, like Newton, as a force, or like Faraday as a field, or like Einstein as a condition in space, gravity was incredibly weak. It was so weak that, although theoretically it was a property of every bit of matter in the universe no matter how small, it could not be worked with in the laboratory. Two magnetized needles will rush toward each other over a distance as great as an inch; so will two balls of pith as small as peas if they bear opposite electrical charges. Two ceramet magnets no bigger than doughnuts can be so strongly charged that it is impossible to push them together by hand when their like poles are opposed, and impossible for a strong man to hold them apart when their unlike poles approach each other. Two spheres of metal of any size, if they bear opposite electrical charges, will mate in a fat spark across the insulating air, if there is no other way that they can neutralize each other.

(But gravity—theoretically one in kind with electricity and magnetism—cannot be charged on to any object. It produces no sparks. There is no such thing as an insulation against it—a di-gravitic. It remains beyond detection as a force, between bodies as small as peas or doughnuts. Two objects as huge as skyscrapers and as massive as lead will take centuries to crawl into the same bed over a foot of distance, if nothing but their mutual gravitational attraction is drawing them together; even love is faster than that. Even a ball of rock eight thousand miles in diameter—the Earth—has a gravitational field too weak to prevent one single man from pole-vaulting away from it to more than four times his own height, driven by no opposing force but that of his spasming muscles.)

"Well, give me a report when you can. If necessary, we can expand." (Is it worth it?)

"I'll give you the report this week." (*Yes!*)

And that was how the Bridge had been born, though nobody had known it then, not even Wagoner. The senators who had investigated the Bridge still didn't know it. MacHinery's staff at the FBI evidently had been unable to penetrate the jargon on their recording of that conversation far enough to connect the conversation with the Bridge; otherwise MacHinery would have given the transcript to the investigators. Mac-Hinery did not exactly love Wagoner; he had been unable thus far to find any handle by which he might grasp and use the Alaskan senator.

All well and good.

And yet the investigators *had* come perilously close, just once. They had subpoenaed Guiseppi Corsi for the preliminary questioning.

Committee Counsel: Now then, Dr. Corsi, according to our records, your last interview with Senator Wagoner

was in the winter of 2013. Did you discuss the Jupiter Project with him at that time?

Corsi: How could I have? It didn't exist then.

Counsel: But was it mentioned to you in any way? Did Senator Wagoner say anything about plans to start such a project?

Corsi: No.

Counsel: You didn't yourself suggest it to Senator Wagoner?

Corsi: Certainly not. It was a total surprise to me, when it was announced afterwards.

Counsel: But I suppose you know what it is.

Corsi: I know only what the general public has been told. We're building a Bridge on Jupiter. It's very costly and ambitious. What it's for is a secret. That's all.

Counsel: You're sure you don't know what it's for?

Corsi: For research.

Counsel: Yes, but research for what? Surely you have some clues.

Corsi: I don't have any clues, and Senator Wagoner didn't give me any. The only facts I have are those I read in the press. Naturally I have some conjectures. But all I *know* is what is indicated, or hinted at, in the official announcements. Those seem to convey the impression that the Bridge is for weapons research.

Counsel: But you think that maybe it isn't?

Corsi: I—I'm not in a position to discuss government projects about which I know nothing.

Counsel: You could give us your opinion.

Corsi: If you want my opinion as an expert, I'll have my office go into the subject and let you know later what such an opinion would cost.

Senator Billings: Dr. Corsi, do we understand that you refuse to answer the question? It seems to me that in

83

view of your past record you might be better advised——

Corsi: I haven't refused to answer, senator. I make part of my living by consultation. If the government wishes to use me in that capacity, it's my right to ask to be paid. You have no right to deprive me of my livelihood, or any part of it.

Senator Croft: The government made up its mind about employing you some time back, Dr. Corsi. And rightly, in my opinion.

Corsi: That is the government's privilege.

Senator Croft: —but you are being questioned now by the Senate of the United States. If you refuse to answer, you may be held in contempt.

Corsi: For refusing to state an opinion?

Counsel: If you will pardon me, Senator Croft, the witness may refuse to offer an opinion—or withhold such an opinion, pending payment. He can be held in contempt only for declining to state the facts, as he knows them.

Senator Croft: All right, let's get some facts, and stop the pussyfooting.

Counsel: Dr. Corsi, was anything said during your last meeting with Senator Wagoner which might have had any bearing on the Jupiter Project?

Corsi: Well, yes. But only negatively. I did counsel him against any such project. Rather emphatically, as I recall.

Counsel: I thought you said that the Bridge hadn't been mentioned.

Corsi: It hadn't. Senator Wagoner and I were discussing research methods in general. I told him that I thought research projects of the Bridge's order of magnitude were no longer fruitful.

84

Senator Billings: Did you charge Senator Wagoner for that opinion, Dr. Corsi?

Corsi: No, senator. Sometimes I don't.

Senator Billings: Perhaps you should have. Wagoner didn't follow your free advice.

Senator Croft: It looks like he considered the source.

Corsi: There's nothing compulsory about advice. I gave him my best opinion at the time. What he did with it was up to him.

Counsel: Would you tell us if that is your best opinion now? That research projects the size of the Bridge are —I believe your phrase was, "no longer fruitful"?

Corsi: That is still my opinion.

Senator Billings: Which you give us free of charge . . . ?

Corsi: It is the opinion of every scientist I know. You could get it free from those who work for you. I have better sense than to charge fees for common knowledge.

It had been a near thing. Perhaps, Wagoner thought, Corsi had after all remembered the really crucial part of that interview, and had decided not to reveal it to the sub-committee. It was more likely, however, that those few words that Corsi had thrown off while standing at the blinded window of his apartment would not have stuck in his memory, as they had stuck in Wagoner's.

Yet surely Corsi knew, at least in part, what the Bridge was for. He must have remembered the part of that conversation which had dealt with gravity. By now he would have reasoned his way from those words all the difficult way to the Bridge—after all, the Bridge was not a difficult object for an understanding like Corsi's.

But he had said nothing about it. That had been a crucial silence.

Wagoner wondered if it would ever be possible for him to show his gratitude to the ageing physicist. Not now. Possibly never. The pain and the puzzlement in Corsi's mind stood forth in what he had said, even over the gap of years, even through the coldness of the official transcript. Wagoner badly wanted to assuage both. But he couldn't. He could only hope that Corsi would see it whole, and understand it whole, when the time came.

The page turned on Corsi. Now there was another question which had to be answered. Was there a single hint, anywhere in the sixteen hundred mimeographed pages of the report, that the Bridge was incomplete without what was going on at Jno. Pfitzner & Sons? . . .

No, there was not. Wagoner let the report fall, with a sigh of relief of which he was hardly conscious. That was that.

He filed the report, and reached into his "In" basket for the dossier on Paige Russell, Colonel, Army Space Corps, which had come in from the Pfitzner plant only a week ago. He was tired, and he did not want to perform an act of judgment on another man for the rest of his life—but he had asked for the job, and now he had to work at it.

Bliss Wagoner had not been cut out to be a general. As a god he was even more inept.

5

It took Paige no more than Anne's mandatory ten seconds, during breakfast of the next day in his snuggery at the Spaceman's Haven, to decide that he was going back to the Pfitzner plant and apologize. He didn't quite understand why the date had ended as catastrophically as it had, but of one thing he was nearly certain: the fiasco had had something to do with his space-rusty manners, and if it were to be mended, he had to be the one to tool up for it.

And now that he came to think of it over his cold egg, it seemed obvious in essence. By his last line of questioning, Paige had broken the delicate shell of the evening and spilled the contents all over the restaurant table. He had left the more or less safe womb of technicalities, and had begun, by implication at least, to call Anne's ethics into question—first by making clear his first reaction to the business about the experimental infants, and then by pressing home her irregular marriage to her firm.

In this world called Earth of disintegrating faiths, one didn't call personal ethical codes into question without getting into trouble. Such codes, where they could be found at all, obviously had cost their adherents too much pain to be open for any new probing. Faith had once been self-evident; now it was desperate. Those who still had it—or had made it, chunk by fragment by shard—wanted nothing but to be allowed to hold it.

As for why he wanted to set matters right with Anne Abbott, Paige was less clear. His leave was passing him by rapidly, and thus far he had done little more than stroll while it passed—especially if he measured it against the desperate meter-stick established by his last two leaves, the two after his marriage had shattered and he had been alone again. After the present leave was over, there was a good chance that he would be assigned to the Proserpine station, which was now about finished and which had no competitors for the title of the most forsaken outpost of the solar system. None, at least, until somebody should discover an 11th planet.

Nevertheless, he was going to go out to the Pfitzner plant again, out to the scenic Bronx, to revel among research scientists, business executives, government brass, and a frozen-voiced girl with a figure like an ironing-board, to kick up his heels on a reception-room rug in the sight of gay steel engravings of the Founders, cheered on by a motto which might or might not be Dionysiac, if he could only read it. Great. Just great. If he played his cards right, he could go on duty at the Proserpine station with fine memories: perhaps the Vice-President in Charge of Export would let Paige call him "Tru", or maybe even "Bubbles".

Maybe it was a matter of religion, after all. Like everyone else in the world, Paige thought, he was still looking for something bigger than himself, bigger than family, Army, marriage, fatherhood, space itself, or the pub-crawls and tyrannically meaningless sexual spasms of a spaceman's leave. Quite obviously the project at Pfitzner, with its air of mystery and selflessness, had touched that very vulnerable nerve in him once more.

Anne Abbott's own dedication was merely the touchstone, the key. . . . . No, he hadn't the right word for it yet, but her attitude somehow fitted into an empty, jagged-edge blemish in his own soul like—like . . . yes, that was it: like a jigsaw-puzzle piece.

And besides, he wanted to see that sunburst smile again.

Because of the way her desk was placed, she was the first thing he saw as he came into Pfitzner's reception room. Her expression was even stranger than he had expected, and she seemed to be making some kind of covert gesture, as though she were flicking dust off the top of her desk toward him with the tips of all her fingers. He took several slower and slower steps into the room and stopped, finally baffled.

Someone rose from a chair which he had not been able to see from the door, and quartered down on him. The pad of the steps on the carpet and the odd crouch of the shape in the corner of Paige's eye were unpleasantly stealthy. Paige turned, unconsciously closing his hands.

"Haven't we seen this officer before, Miss Abbott? What's his business here—or has he any?"

The man in the eager semi-crouch was Francis X. MacHinery.

Like his unforgettable grandfather, Francis X. MacHinery was a beetle-browed, heavy-faced man who seemed always in need of a shave. Though he would have been easy to dismiss on first glance as a not very bright truck driver, MacHinery was as full of cunning as a wolverine, and he had managed times without number to land on his feet regardless of what political disasters had been planned for him. And he was, as Paige was now discovering, the man for whom the metaphor "gimlet-eyed" had all unknowingly been invented.

"Well, Miss Abbott?"

"Colonel Russell was here yesterday," Anne said. "You may have seen him then."

The swinging doors opened and Horsefield and Gunn came in. MacHinery paid no attention to them. He said: "What's your name, soldier?"

"I'm a spaceman," Paige said stiffly. "Colonel Paige Russell, Army Space Corps."

"What are you doing here?"

"I'm on leave."

"Will you answer the question?" MacHinery said. He was, Paige noticed, not looking at Paige at all, but over his shoulder, as though he were actually paying no real heed to the conversation. "What are you doing at the Pfitzner plant?"

"I happen to be in love with Miss Abbott," Paige said sharply, to his own black and utter astonishment. "I came here to see her. We had a quarrel last night and I wanted to apologize. That's all."

Anne straightened behind her desk as though a curtain rod had been driven up her spine, turning toward Paige a pair of blindly blazing eyes and a rigidly unreadable expression. Even Gunn's mouth sagged slightly to one side; he looked first at Anne, then at Paige, as if he were abruptly uncertain that he had ever seen either of them before.

MacHinery, however, shot only one quick look at Anne, and his eyes seemed to turn into bottle-glass. "I'm not interested in your personal life," he said, in a tone which, indeed, suggested active boredom. "I will put the question another way, so that there'll be no excuse for evading it. Why did you come to the plant in the first place? What is your *business* at Pfitzner, soldier?"

Paige tried to pick his next words carefully. Actually it would hardly matter what he said, once MacHinery developed a real interest in him; an accusation from the FBI had nearly the force of law. Everything depended upon so conducting himself as to be of no interest to MacHinery to begin with—an exercise at which, fortunately up to now, Paige had had no more practice than had any other spaceman.

He said: "I brought in some soil samples from the Jovian system. Pfitzner asked me to do it, as part of their research programme."

"And you brought these samples in yesterday, you told me."

"No, I didn't tell you. But as a matter of fact I did bring them in yesterday."

"And you're still bringing them in today, I see." MacHinery jerked his chin over his shoulder toward Horsefield, whose face had frozen into complete tetany as soon as he had shown signs of realizing what was going on. "What about this, Horsefield? Is this one of your men that you haven't told me about?"

"No," Horsefield said, but putting a sort of a question-mark into the way he spoke the word, as though he did not mean to deny anything which he might later be expected to affirm. "Saw the man yesterday, I think. For the first time, to the best of my knowledge."

"I see. Would you say, General, that this man is no part of the Army's assigned complement on the project?"

"I can't say that for sure," Horsefield said, his voice sounding more positive now that he was voicing a doubt. "I'd have to consult my T.O. Perhaps he's somebody new in Alsos' group. He's not part of my staff, though—doesn't claim that he is, does he?"

"Gunn, what about this man? Did you people take him on without checking with me? Does he have security clearance?"

"Well, we did in a way, but he didn't need to be cleared," Gunn said. "He's just a field collector, hasn't any real part in the research work, no official connection. These field people are all volunteers; you know that."

MacHinery's brows were drawing closer and closer together. With only a few more of these questions, Paige knew even from the few newspapers which had reached him in space, he would have material enough for an arrest and a sensation—the kind of sensation which would pillory Pfitzner, destroy every civilian working for Pfitzner, trigger a long chain of courts martial among the military assignees, ruin the politicians who had sponsored the research, and thicken MacHinery's scrapbook of headlines about himself by at least three inches. That last outcome was the only one in which MacHinery was really interested; that the project itself would die was a side-effect which, though nearly inevitable, could hardly have interested him less.

"Excuse me, Mr. Gunn," Anne said quietly. "I don't think you're quite as familiar with Colonel Russell's status as I am. He's just come in from deep space, and his security record has been in the 'Clean and Routine' file for years; he's not one of our ordinary field collectors."

"Ah," Gunn said. "I'd forgotten, but that's quite true." Since it was both true and perfectly irrelevant, Paige could not understand why Gunn was quite so hearty about agreeing to it. Did he think Anne was stalling?

"As a matter of fact," Anne proceeded steadily,

"Colonel Russell is a planetary ecologist specializing in the satellites; he's been doing important work for us. He's quite well known in space, and has many friends on the Bridge team and elsewhere. That's correct, isn't it, Colonel Russell?"

"I know most of the Bridge gang," Paige agreed, but he barely managed to make his assent audible. What the girl was saying added up to something very like a big, black lie. And lying to MacHinery was a short cut to ruin; only MacHinery had the privilege of lying, never his witnesses.

"The samples Colonel Russell brought us yesterday contained crucial material," Anne said. "That's why I asked him to come back; we needed his advice. And if his samples turn out to be as important as they seem, they'll save the taxpayer quite a lot of money—they may help us close out the project a long time in advance of the projected closing date. If that's to be possible, Colonel Russell will have to guide the last steps of the work personally; he's the only one who knows the microflora of the Jovian satellites well enough to interpret the results."

MacHinery looked dubiously over Paige's shoulder. It was hard to tell whether or not he had heard a word. Nevertheless, it was evident that Anne had chosen her final approach with great care, for if MacHinery had any weakness at all, it was the enormous cost of his continual, overlapping investigations. Lately he had begun to be nearly as sure death on "waste in government" as he was traditionally on "subversives". He said at last:

"There's obviously something irregular here. If all that's so, why did the man say what he said in the beginning?"

"Perhaps because it's also true," Paige said sharply.

93

MacHinery ignored him. "We'll check the records and call anyone we need. Horsefield, let's go."

The general trailed him out, his back very stiff, after a glare at Paige which failed to be in the least convincing, and an outrageously stagey wink at Anne. The moment the outer door closed behind the two, the reception-room seemed to explode. Gunn swung on Anne with a motion astonishingly tiger-like for so mild-faced a man. Anne was already rising from behind her desk, her face twisted with fear and fury. Both of them were shouting at once.

"Now see what you've done with your damned nosiness——"

"What in the world did you want to tell MacHinery a tale like that for——"

"—even a spaceman should know better than to hang around a defence area——"

"—you know as well as I do that those Ganymede samples are trash——"

"—you've probably cost us our whole appropriation with your snooping——"

"—we've never hired a 'Clean and Routine' man since the project began——"

"—I hope you're satisfied——"

"—I would have thought you'd have better sense by now——"

"*Quiet!*" Paige shouted over them, with the authentic parade-ground blare. He had never found any use for it in deep space, but it worked now. Both of them looked at him, their mouths still incongruously half-opened, their faces white as milk. "You act like a pair of hysterical chickens, both of you! I'm sorry if I got you into trouble—but I didn't ask Anne to lie in my behalf—and I didn't ask you to go along with it, either,

94

Gunn! Maybe you'd best stop yelling accusations and try to think the thing through. I'll try to help, for whatever that's worth—but not if you're going to scream and weep at each other and at me!"

The girl bared her teeth at him in a real snarl, the first time he had ever seen a human being mount such an expression and mean it. She sat down, however, swiping at her patchily red cheeks with a piece of cleansing tissue. Gunn looked down at the carpet and just breathed noisily for a moment, putting the palms of his hands together solemnly before his white lips.

"I quite agree," Gunn said after a moment, as calmly as if nothing had happened. "We'll have to get to work and work fast. Anne, please tell me: why was it necessary for you to say that Colonel Russell was essential to the project? I'm not accusing you of anything, but we need to know the facts."

"I went to dinner with Colonel Russell last night," Anne said. "I was somewhat indiscreet about the project. At the end of the evening we had a quarrel which was probably overheard by at least two of MacHinery's amateur informers in the restaurant. I had to lie for my own protection, as well as Colonel Russell's."

"But you have an Eavesdropper! If you knew that you might be overheard——"

"I knew it well enough. But I lost my temper. You know how these things go."

It all came out as emotionlessly as a tape recording. Told in these terms, the incident sounded to Paige like something that had happened to someone whom he had never met, whose name he could not even pronounce with certainty. Only the fact that Anne's eyes were reddened with furious tears offered any bridge between the cold narrative and the charged memory.

"Yes; nasty," Gunn said reflectively. "Colonel Russell, *do* you know the Bridge team?"

"I know some of them quite well, Charity Dillon in particular; after all, I was stationed in the Jovian system for a while. MacHinery's check will show that I've no official connection with the Bridge, however."

"Good, good," Gunn said, beginning to brighten. "That widens MacHinery's check to include the Bridge too, and dilutes it from Pfitzner's point of view—gives us more time, though I'm sorry for the Bridge men. The Bridge and the Pfitzner project both suspect—yes, that's a big mouthful even for MacHinery; it will take him months. And the Bridge is Senator Wagoner's pet project, so he'll have to go slowly; he can't assassinate Wagoner's reputation as rapidly as he could some other senator's. Hmm. The question now is, just how are we going to use the time?"

"When you calm down, you calm right down to the bottom," Paige said, grinning wryly.

"I'm a salesman," Gunn said. "Maybe more creative than some, but at heart a salesman. In that profession you have to suit the mood to the occasion, just like actors do. Now about those samples——"

"I shouldn't have thrown that in," Anne said. "I'm afraid it was one good touch too many."

"On the contrary, it may be the only out we have. MacHinery is a 'practical' man. Results are what count with him. So suppose we take Colonel Russell's samples out of the regular testing order and run them through right now, issuing special orders to the staff that they are to find something in them—anything that looks at all decent."

"The staff won't fake," Anne said, frowning.

"My dear Anne, who said anything about faking?

Nearly every batch of samples contains some organism of interest, even if it isn't good enough to wind up among our choicest cultures. You see? MacHinery will be contented by results if we can show them to him, even though the results may have been made possible by an unauthorized person; otherwise he'd have to assemble a committee of experts to assess the evidence, and that costs money. All this, of course, is predicated on whether or not we have any results by the time MacHinery finds out Colonel Russell *is* an unauthorized person."

"There's just one other thing," Anne said. "To make good on what I told MacHinery, we're going to have to turn Colonel Russell into a convincing planetary ecologist—*and* tell him just what the Pfitzner project is."

Gunn's face fell momentarily. "Anne," he said, "I want you to observe what a nasty situation that strong-arm man has gotten us into. In order to protect our legitimate interests from our own government, we're about to commit a real, serious breach of security—which would never have happened if MacHinery hadn't thrown his weight around."

"Quite true," Anne said. She looked, however, rather poker-faced, Paige thought. Possibly she was enjoying Gunn's discomfiture; he was not exactly the first man one would suspect of disloyalty or of being a security risk.

"Colonel Russell, there is no faint chance, I suppose, that you *are* a planetary ecologist? Most spacemen with ranks as high as yours are scientists of some kind."

"No, sorry," Paige said. "Ballistics is my field."

"Well, you do have to know something about the planets, at least. Anne, I suggest that you take charge now, I'll have to do some fast covering. Your father would probably be the best man to brief Colonel Russell. And, Colonel, would you bear in mind that from now on, every piece of information that you're given in our plant might have the giver jailed or even shot, if MacHinery were to find out about it?"

"I'll keep my mouth shut," Paige said. "I'm enough at fault in this mess to be willing to do all I can to help —and my curiosity has been killing me anyhow. But there's something you'd better know, too, Mr. Gunn."

"And that is——"

"That the time you're counting on just doesn't exist. My leave expires in ten days. If you think you can make a planetary ecologist out of me in that length of time, I'll do my part."

"Ulp," Gunn said. "Anne, get to work." He bolted through the swinging doors.

The two looked at each other for a starchy moment, and then Anne smiled. Paige felt like another man at once.

"Is it really true—what you said?" Anne said, almost shyly.

"Yes. I didn't know it until I said it, but it's true. I'm really sorry that I had to say it at such a spectacularly bad moment; I only came over to apologize for my part in last night's quarrel. Now it seems that I've a bigger hassel to account for."

"Your curiosity is really your major talent, do you know?" she said, smiling again. "It took you only two days to find out just what you wanted to know—even though it's about the most closely guarded secret in the world."

"But I don't know it yet. Can you tell me here—or is the place wired?"

The girl laughed. "Do you think Tru and I would

98

have cussed each other out like that if the place were wired? No, it's clean, we inspect it daily. I'll tell you the central fact, and then my father can give you the details. The truth is that the Pfitzner project isn't out to conquer the degenerative diseases alone. It's aimed at the end-product of those diseases, too. *We're looking for the answer to death itself.*"

Paige sat down slowly in the nearest chair. "I don't believe it can be done," he whispered at last.

"That's what we all used to think, Paige. That's what that says." She pointed to the motto in German above the swinging doors. "*Wider den Tod ist kein Krautlein gewachsen.*" " 'Against Death doth no simple grow.' That was a law of nature, the old German herbalists thought. But now it's only a challenge. Somewhere in nature there *are* herbs and simples against death—and we're going to find them."

Anne's father seemed both preoccupied and a little worried to be talking to Paige at all, but it nevertheless took him only one day to explain the basic reasoning behind the project vividly enough so that Paige could understand it. In another day of simple helping around the part of the Pfitzner labs which was running his soil samples—help which consisted mostly of bottle-washing and making dilutions—Paige learned the reasoning well enough to put forward a version of it himself. He practised it on Anne over dinner.

"It all rests on our way of thinking about why antibiotics work," he said, while the girl listened with an attentiveness just this side of mockery. "What good are they to the organisms that produce them? We assumed that the organism secretes the antibiotic to kill or inhibit competing organisms, even though we were never able to show that enough antibiotic for the purpose is actually produced in the organism's natural medium, that is, the soil. In other words, we figured, the wider the range of the antibiotic, the less competition the producer had."

"Watch out for teleology," Anne warned. "That's not *why* the organism secretes it. It's just the result. Function, not purpose."

"Fair enough. But right there is the borderline in our thinking about antibiosis. What is an antibiotic to the organism it *kills*? Obviously, it's a poison, a toxin. But some bacteria always are naturally resistant to a given antibiotic, and through—what did your father call it?— through clone-variation and selection, the resistant cells may take over a whole colony. Equally obviously, those resistant cells would seem to produce an anti-toxin. An example would be the bacteria that secrete penicillinase, which is an enzyme that destroys penicillin. To those bacteria, penicillin is a toxin, and penicillinase is an antitoxin—isn't that right?"

"Right as rain. Go on, Paige."

"So now we add to that still another fact: that both penicillin and tetracycline are not only antibiotics— which makes them toxic to many bacteria—but *antitoxins* as well. Both of them neutralize the placental toxin that causes the eclampsia of pregnancy. Now, tetracycline is a broad-range antibiotic; is there such a thing as a broad-range antitoxin, too? Is the resistance to tetracycline that many different kinds of bacteria can develop all derived from a single counteracting substance? The answer, we know now, is Yes. We've also found another kind of broad-range antitoxin—one which protects the organism against many different kinds of antibiotics. I'm told that it's a whole new field of research and that we've just begun to scratch the surface.

"Ergo: Find the broad-range antitoxin that acts against the toxins of the human body which accumulate after growth stops—as penicillin and tetracycline act against the pregnancy toxin—and you've got your magic machine-gun against degenerative disease. Pfitzner already has found that antitoxin: its name is ascomycin. . . . How'd I do?" he added anxiously, getting his breath back.

"Beautifully. It's perhaps a little too condensed for MacHinery to follow, but maybe that's all to the good —it wouldn't sound authoritative to him if he could understand it all the way through. Still it might pay to be just a little more roundabout when you talk to him." The girl had the compact out again, and was peering into it intently. "But you covered only the degenerative diseases, and that's just background material. Now tell me about the direct attack on death."

Paige looked at the compact and then at the girl, but her expression was too studied to convey much. He said slowly: "I'll go into that if you like. But your father told me that that element of the work was secret even from the government. Should I discuss it in a restaurant?"

Anne turned the small, compact-like object around, so that he could see that it was in fact a meter of some sort. Its needle was in uncertain motion, but near the zero-point. "There's no mike close enough to pick you up," Anne said, snapping the device shut and restoring it to her purse. "Go ahead."

"All right. Some day you're going to have to explain to me why you allowed yourself to get into that first fight with me here, when you had that Eavesdropper with you all the time. Right at the moment I'm too busy being a phony ecologist.

"The death end of the research began back in 1952, with an anatomist named Lansing. He was the first man to show that complex animals—it was rotifers he used—produce a definite ageing toxin as a normal part of their growth, and that it gets passed on to the offspring. He bred something like fifty generations of rotifers from adolescent mothers, and got an increase in the life-span in every new generation. He ran 'em up from a natural average span of 24 days to one of 104 days. Then he reversed the process, by breeding consistently from old mothers, and cut the life-span of the final generation way *below* the natural average."

"And now," Anne said, "you know more about the babies in our labs than I told you before—or you should. The foundling home that supplies them specializes in the illegitimates of juvenile delinquents—the younger, for our purposes, the better."

"Sorry, but you can't needle me with that any longer, Anne. I know now that it's a blind alley. Breeding for longevity in humans isn't practicable; all that those infants can supply to the project is a set of comparative readings on their death-toxin blood-levels. What we want now is something much more direct: an antitoxin against the ageing toxin of humans. We know that the ageing toxin exists in all complex animals. We know that it's a single, specific substance, quite distinct from the poisons that cause the degenerative diseases. And we know that it can be neutralized. When your lab animals were given ascomycin, they didn't develop a single degenerative disease—but they died anyhow, at about the usual time, as if they'd been set, like a clock, at birth. Which, in effect, they had, by the amount of ageing toxin passed on to them by their mothers.

"So what we're looking for now is not an antibiotic—an anti-life drug—but an anti-agathic, an anti-death drug. We're running on borrowed time, because ascomycin already satisfies the conditions of our development contract with the government. As soon as we get ascomycin into production, our government money will be cut down to a trickle. But if we can hold back on ascomycin long enough to keep the money coming in, we'll have our anti-agathic too."

"Bravo," Anne said. "You sound just like father. I wanted you to raise that last point in particular, Paige, because it's the most important single thing you should remember. If there's the slightest suspicion that we're systematically dragging our feet on releasing ascomycin —that we're taking money from the government to do something the government has no idea can be done— there'll be hell to pay. We're so close to running down our anti-agathic now that it would be heart-breaking to have to stop, not only heart-breaking for us, but for humanity at large."

"The end justifies the means," Paige murmured.

"It does in this case. I know secrecy's a fetish in our society these days—but here secrecy will serve everyone in the long run, and it's *got* to be maintained."

"I'll maintain it," Paige said. He had been referring, not to secrecy, but to cheating on government money; but he saw no point in bringing that up. As for secrecy, he had no practical faith in it—especially now that he had seen how well it worked.

For in the two days that he had been working inside Pfitzner, he had already found an inarguable spy at the very heart of the project.

103

6

There were three yellow "Critical" signals lit on the long gangboard when Helmuth passed through the gang deck on the way back to duty. All of them, as usual, were concentrated on Panel 9, where Eva Chavez worked.

Eva, despite her Latin name—such once-valid tickets no longer meant anything among the West's uniformly mixed-race population—was a big girl, vaguely blonde, who cherished a passion for the Bridge. Unfortunately, she was apt to become enthralled by the sheer Cosmicness of It All, precisely at the moment when cold analysis and split-second decisions were most crucial.

Helmuth reached over her shoulder, cut her out of the circuit except as an observer, and donned the co-operator's helmet. The incomplete new shoals caisson sprang into being around him. Breakers of boiling hydrogen seethed seven hundred feet up along its slanted sides—breakers that never subsided, but simply were torn away into flying spray.

There was a spot of dull orange near the top of the north face of the caisson, crawling slowly toward the pediment of the nearest truss. Catalysis——

Or cancer, as Helmuth could not help but think of it. On this bitter, violent monster of a planet, even tiny specks of calcium carbide were deadly, that same calcium carbide which had produced acetylene gas for buggy lamps two centuries ago on Earth. At these wind velocities, such specks imbedded themselves deeply in anything they struck; and at fifteen million p.s.i of pressure, under the catalysis of sodium, pressure-ice took up ammonia and carbon dioxide, building protein-like compounds in a rapid, voracious chain of decay:

For a moment, Helmuth watched it grow. It was, after all, one of the incredible possibilities the Bridge had been built to study. On Earth, such a compound, had it occurred at all, might have grown porous, hard, and as strong as rhinocerous-horn. Here, under nearly three times Earth's gravity, the molecules were forced to assemble in strict aliphatic order, but in cross section their arrangement was hexagonal, as though the stuff would become an aromatic compound if only it could. Even here it was moderately strong in cross section—

but along the long axis it smeared like graphite, the calcium and sulphur atoms readily changing their minds as to which was to act as the metal of the pair, surrendering their pressure-driven holds on one carbon atom to grab hopefully for the next one in line, or giving up altogether to become incorporated instead in a radical with a self-contained double sulphur bond, rather like cystine. . . .

It was not too far from the truth to call it a form of cancer. The compound seemed to be as close as Jupiter came to an indigenous form of life. It grew, fed, reproduced itself, and showed something of the characteristic structure of an Earthly virus, such as tobacco-mosaic. Of course it grew from outside, by accretion like any non-living crystal, rather than from inside, by intussusception, like a cell; but viruses grew that way too, at least *in vitro*.

It was no stuff to hold up the piers of humanity's greatest engineering project, that much was sure. Perhaps it was a suitable ground-substance for the ribs of some Jovian jellyfish; but in a Bridge-caisson, it was cancer.

There was a scraper mechanism working on the edge of the lesion, flaking away the shearing aminos and laying down new ice. In the meantime, the decay in the caisson-face was working deeper. The scraper could not possibly get at the core of the trouble—which was not the calcium carbide dust, with which the atmosphere was charged beyond redemption, but was instead one imbedded speck of metallic sodium which was taking no part in the reaction—fast enough to extirpate it. It could barely keep pace with the surface spread of the disease.

And laying new ice over the surface of the wound was

worthless, as Eva should have known. At this rate, the whole caisson would slough away and melt like butter, within an hour, under the weight of the Bridge above it.

Helmuth sent the futile scraper aloft. Drill for the speck of metal? No—it was far too deeply buried already, and its location was unknown.

Quickly he called two borers up from the shoals below, where constant blasting was taking the foundation of the caisson deeper and deeper into Jupiter's dubious "soil". He drove both blind, fire-snouted machines down into the lesion.

The bottom of that sore turned out to be forty-five metres within the immense block of ice. Helmuth pushed the red button all the same.

The borers blew up, with a heavy, quite invisible blast, as they had been designed to do. A pit appeared on the face of the caisson.

The nearest truss bent upward in the wind. It fluttered for a moment, trying to resist. It bent farther.

Deprived of its major attachment, it tore free suddenly, and went whirling away into the blackness. A sudden flash of lightning picked it out for a moment, and Helmuth saw it dwindling like a bat with torn wings being borne away by a cyclone.

The scraper scuttled down into the pit and began to fill it with ice from the bottom. Helmuth ordered down a new truss and a squad of scaffolders. Damage of this order of magnitude took time to repair. He watched the tornado tearing ragged chunks from the edges of the pit until he was sure that the catalysis-cancer had been stopped. Then—suddenly, prematurely, dismally tired —he took off the helmet.

He was astounded by the white fury that masked Eva's big-boned, mildly pretty face.

"You'll blow the Bridge up yet, won't you?" she said, evenly, without preamble. "Any pretext will do!"

Baffled, Helmuth turned his head helplessly away; but that was no better. The suffused face of Jupiter peered swollenly through the picture-port, just as it did on the foreman's deck.

He and Eva and Charity and the gang and the whole of satellite V were falling forward toward Jupiter; their uneventful, cooped-up lives on Jupiter V were utterly unreal compared to the four hours of each changeless day spent on Jupiter's ever-changing surface. Every new day brought their minds, like ships out of control, closer and closer to that gaudy inferno.

There was no other way for a man—or a woman—on Jupiter V to look at the giant planet. It was simple experience, shared by all of them, that planets do not occupy four-fifths of the whole sky, unless the observer is himself up there in that planet's sky, falling toward it, falling faster and faster——

"I have no intention," he said tiredly, "of blowing up the Bridge. I wish you could get it through your head that I want the Bridge to stay up—even though I'm not starry-eyed to the point of incompetence about the project. Did you think that that rotten spot was going to go away by itself after you'd painted it over? Didn't you know that——"

Several helmeted, masked heads near by turned blindly toward the sound of his voice. Helmuth shut up. Any distracting conversation or other activity was taboo, down here on the gang deck. He motioned Eva back to duty.

The girl donned her helmet obediently enough, but it was plain from the way that her normally full lips were thinned that she thought Helmuth had ended the argument only in order to have the last word.

Helmuth strode to the thick pillar which ran down the central axis of the operations shack, and mounted the spiralling cleats toward his own foreman's cubicle. Already he felt in anticipation the weight of the helmet upon his own head.

Charity Dillon, however, was already wearing the helmet. He was sitting in Helmuth's chair.

Charity was characteristically oblivious of Helmuth's entrance. The Bridge operator must learn to ignore, to be utterly unconscious of anything happening about his body except the inhuman sounds of signals; must learn to heed only those senses which report something going on thousands and hundreds of thousands of miles away.

Helmuth knew better than to interrupt him. Instead, he watched Dillon's white, blade-like fingers roving with blind sureness over the controls.

Dillon, evidently, was making a complete tour of the Bridge—not only from end to end, but up and down, too. The tally board showed that he had already activated nearly two-thirds of the ultraphone eyes. That meant that he had been up all night at the job; had begun it immediately after he had last relieved Helmuth.

Why?

With a thrill of unfocused apprehension, Helmuth looked at the foreman's jack, which allowed the operator here in the cubicle to communicate with the gang when necessary, and which kept him aware of anything said or done on the gang boards.

It was plugged in.

Dillon sighed suddenly, took the helmet off, and turned.

"Hello, Bob," he said. "It's funny about this job. You can't see, you can't hear, but when somebody's watching you, you feel a sort of pressure on the back of your neck. Extra-sensory perception, maybe. Ever felt it?"

"Pretty often, lately. Why the grand tour, Charity?"

"There's to be an inspection," Dillon said. His eyes met Helmuth's. They were frank and transparent. "A couple of Senate sub-committee chairmen, coming to see that their eight billion dollars isn't being wasted. Naturally, I'm a little anxious to see to it that they find everything in order."

"I see," Helmuth said. "First time in five years, isn't it?"

"Just about. What was that dust-up down below just now? Somebody—you, I'm sure, from the drastic handiwork involved—bailed Eva out of a mess, and then I heard her talk about your wanting to blow up the Bridge. I checked the area when I heard the fracas start, and it did seem as if she had let things go rather far, but—— What was it all about?"

Dillon ordinarily hadn't the guile for cat-and-mouse games, and he had never looked less guileful than now. Helmuth said carefully: "Eva was upset, I suppose. On the subject of Jupiter we're all of us cracked by now, in our different ways. The way she was dealing with the catalysis didn't look to me to be suitable—a difference of opinion, resolved in my favour because I had the authority, Eva didn't. That's all."

"Kind of an expensive difference, Bob. I'm not niggling by nature, you know that. But an incident like that while the sub-committees are here——"

"The point is," said Helmuth, "are we going to spend an extra ten thousand, or whatever it costs to replace a truss and reinforce a caisson, or are we to lose the whole caisson—and as much as a third of the whole Bridge along with it?"

"Yes, you're right there, of course. That could be explained, even to a pack of senators. But—it would be difficult to have to explain it very often. Well, the board's yours, Bob; you could continue my spot-check, if you've time."

Dillon got up. Then he added suddenly, as though it were forced out of him:

"Bob, I'm trying to understand your state of mind. From what Eva said, I gather that you've made it fairly public. I . . . I don't think it's a good idea to infect your fellow workers with your own pessimism. It leads to sloppy work. I know that you won't countenance sloppy work, regardless of your own feelings, but one foreman can do only so much. And you're making extra work for yourself—not for me, but for yourself—by being openly gloomy about the Bridge.

"It strikes me that maybe you could use a breather, maybe a week's junket to Ganymede or something like that. You're the best man on the Bridge, Bob, for all your grousing about the job, and your assorted misgivings. I'd hate to see you replaced."

"A threat, Charity?" Helmuth said softly.

"*No*. I wouldn't replace you unless you actually went nuts, and I firmly believe that your fears in that respect are groundless. It's a commonplace that only sane men suspect their own sanity, isn't it?"

"It's a common misconception. Most psychopathic obsessions begin with a mild worry—one that can't be shaken."

Dillon made as if to brush that subject away. "Anyhow, I'm not threatening; I'd fight to keep you here.

III

But my say-so only covers Jupiter V and the Bridge; there are people higher up on Ganymede, and people higher yet back in Washington—and in this inspecting commission.

"Why don't you try to look on the bright side for a change? Obviously the Bridge isn't ever going to inspire you. But you might at least try thinking about all those dollars piling up in your account back home, every hour you're on this job. And about the bridges and ships and who knows what-all that you'll be building, at any fee you ask, when you get back down to Earth. All under the magic words: 'One of the men who built the Bridge on Jupiter'!"

Charity was bright red with embarrassment and enthusiasm. Helmuth smiled.

"I'll try to bear it in mind, Charity," he said. "And I think I'll pass up a vacation for the time being. When is this gaggle of senators due to arrive?"

"That's hard to say. They'll be coming to Ganymede directly from Washington, without any routing, and they'll stop there a while. I suppose they'll also make a stop at Callisto before they come here. They've got something new on their ship, I'm told, that lets them flit about more freely than the usual uphill transport can."

An icy lizard suddenly was nesting in Helmuth's stomach, coiling and coiling but never settling itself. The persistent nightmare began to seep back into his blood; it was almost engulfing him—already.

"Something . . . new?" he echoed, his voice as flat and non-committal as he could make it. "Do you know what it is?"

"Well, yes. But I think I'd better keep quiet about it until——"

"Charity, nobody on this deserted rock-heap could possibly be a Soviet spy. The whole habit of 'security' is idiotic out here. Tell me now and save me the trouble of dealing with senators; or tell me at least that you know I know. *They have antigravity!* Isn't that it?"

One word from Dillon, and the nightmare would be real.

"Yes," Dillon said. "How did you know? Of course, it couldn't be a complete gravity screen by any means. But it seems to be a good long step toward it. We've waited a long time to see that dream come true——

"But you're the last man in the world to take pride in the achievement, so there's no sense in exulting about it to you. I'll let you know when I get a definite arrival date. In the meantime, will you think about what I said before?"

"Yes, I will." Helmuth took the seat before the board.

"Good. With you, I have to be grateful for small victories. Good trick, Bob."

"Good trick, Charity."

7

Paige's gift for putting two and two together and getting 22 was in part responsible for the discovery of the spy, but the almost incredible clumsiness of the man made the chief contribution to it. Paige could hardly believe that nobody had spotted the agent before. True, he was only one of some two dozen technicians in the processing lab where Paige had been working; but his almost open habit of slipping notes inside his lab apron, and his painful furtiveness every time he left the Pfitzner laboratory building for the night, should have aroused someone's suspicions long before this.

It was a fine example, Paige thought, of the way the blunderbus investigation methods currently popular in Washington allowed the really dangerous man a thousand opportunities to slip away unnoticed. As was usual among groups of scientists, too, there was an unspoken covenant among Pfitzner's technicians—against informing on each other. It protected the guilty as well as the innocent, but it would never have arisen at all under any fair system of juridical defence.

Paige had not the smallest idea what to do with his fish once he had hooked it. He took an evening—which he greatly begrudged—away from seeing Anne, in order to trace the man's movements after a day which had produced two exciting advances in the research, on the hunch that the spy would want to ferry the information out at once.

This hunch proved out beautifully, at least at first. Nor was the man difficult to follow; his habit of glancing continually over first one shoulder and then the other, evidently to make sure that he was not being followed, made him easy to spot over long distances, even in a crowd. He left the city by train to Hoboken, where he rented a bicycle and pedalled directly to the cross-roads town of Secaucus, which called itself—accurately, to judge by the smell—"The Biggest Little Piggery On Earth". It was a long pull, but not at all difficult otherwise.

Outside Secaucus, however, Paige nearly lost his man for the first and last time. The cross-roads, which lay across New Jersey Route 3 to the Lincoln Tunnel, turned out also to be the site of the temporary trailer city of the Witnesses—nearly 300,000 of them, or almost half of the 700,000 who had been pouring into town for two weeks now for the Revival. Among the trailers Paige saw licence plates from as far away as Eritrea.

The trailer city was far bigger than any nearby town except Passaic. It included a score of supermarkets, all going full blast even in the middle of the night, and about as many coin-in-slot laundries, equally wide open. There were at least a hundred public baths, and close to 360 public toilets. Paige counted ten cafeterias, and twice that many hamburger stands and one-arm joints, each of the stands no less than a hundred feet long; at one of these he stopped long enough to buy a "Texas wiener" nearly as long as his forearm, covered with mustard, meat sauce, sauerkraut, corn relish, and piccalilli. There were ten highly conspicuous hospital tents, too—and after eating the Texas wiener Paige thought he knew why—the smallest of them perfectly capable of housing a one-ring circus.

And, of course, there were the trailers, of which Paige guessed the number at sixty thousand, from two-wheeled jobs to Packards, in all stages of repair and shininess. Luckily, the city was well lit, and since everyone living in it was a Witness, there were no booby-traps or other forms of proselytizing. Paige's man, after a little thoroughly elementary doubling on his tracks and setting up false trails, ducked into a trailer with a Latvian licence plate. After half an hour—at exactly 0200—the trailer ran up a stubby VHF radio antenna as thick through as Paige's wrist.

And the rest, Paige thought grimly, climbing back on to his own rented bicycle, is up to the FBI—if I tell them.

But what would he say? He had every good reason of his own to stay as far out of sight of the FBI as possible. Furthermore, if he informed on the man now, it would mean immediate curtains on the search for the anti-agathic, and a gross betrayal of the trust, enforced though it had been, that Anne and Gunn had placed in him. On the other hand, to remain silent would give the Soviets the drug at the same time that Pfitzner found it—in other words, before the West had it as a government. And it would mean, too, that he himself would have to forego an important chance to prove that he was loyal, when the inevitable showdown with Mac-Hinery came around.

By the next day, however, he had hit upon what should have been the obvious course in the beginning. He took a second evening to rifle his fish's laboratory bench—the incredible idiot had stuffed it to bulging with incriminating photomicrograph negatives, and with bits of paper bearing the symbols of a simple substitution code once circulated to Tom Mix's Square Shooters on behalf of Shredded Ralston—and a third to take step-by-step photos of the hegira to the Witness trailer city, and of the radio-transmitter-equipped trailer with the buffer-state licence. Assembling everything into a neat dossier, Paige cornered Gunn in his office and dropped the whole mess squarely in the vice-president's lap.

"My goodness," Gunn said, blinking. "Curiosity is a disease with you, isn't it, Colonel Russell? And I really doubt that even Pfitzner will ever find the antidote for that."

"Curiosity has very little to do with it. As you'll see in the folder, the man's an amateur—evidently a volunteer from the Party, like the Rosenbergs, rather than a paid expert. He practically led me by the nose."

"Yes, I see he's clumsy," Gunn agreed. "And he's been reported to us before, Colonel Russell. As a matter of fact, on several occasions we've had to protect him from his own clumsiness."

"But why?" Paige demanded. "Why haven't you cracked down on him?"

"Because we can't afford to," Gunn said. "A spy scandal in the plant now would kill the work just where it stands. Oh, we'll report him sooner or later, and the work you've done here on him will be very useful then —to all of us, yourself included. But there's no hurry."

"No hurry!"

"No," Gunn said. "The material he's ferrying out now is of no particular consequence. When we actually have the drug——"

"But he'll already know the production method by that time. Identifying the drug is a routine job for any team of chemists—your Dr. Agnew taught me that much."

"I suppose that's so," Gunn said. "Well, I'll think it over, Colonel. Don't worry about it, we'll deal with it when the time seems ripe."

And that was every bit of satisfaction that Paige could extract from Gunn. It was small recompense for his lost sleep, his lost dates, the care he had taken to inform Pfitzner first, or the soul-searching it had cost him to put the interests of the project ahead of his officer's oath and of his own safety. That evening he said as much to Anne Abbott, and with considerable force.

"Calm down," Anne said. "If you're going to mix into the politics of this work, Paige, you're going to get burnt right up to the armpits. When we do find what we're looking for, it's going to create the biggest political explosion in history. I'd advise you to stand well back."

"I've been burned already," Paige said hotly. "How the hell can I stand back now? And tolerating a spy isn't just politics. It's treason, not only by rumour, but in fact. Are you deliberately putting everyone's head in the noose?"

"Quite deliberately. Paige, this project is for everyone—every man, woman and child on the Earth and in space. The fact that the West is putting up the money is incidental. What we're doing here is in every respect just as anti-West as it is anti-Soviet. We're out to lick death for human beings, not just for the armed forces of some one military coalition. What do we care who gets it first? We want everyone to have it."

"Does Gunn agree with that?"

"It's company policy. It may even have been Tru's own idea, though he has different reasons, different

118

justifications. Have you any idea what will happen when a death-curing drug hits a totalitarian society—a drug available in limited quantities only? It won't prove fatal to the Soviets, of course, but it ought to make the struggle for succession over there considerably bloodier than it is already. That's essentially the way Tru seems to look at it."

"And you don't," Paige said grimly.

"No, Paige, I don't. I can see well enough what's going to happen right here at home when this thing gets out. Think for a moment of what it will do to the religious people alone. What happens to the after-life if you never need to leave this one? Look at the Witnesses. They believe in the literal truth of everything in the Bible—that's why they revise the book every year. And this story is going to break before their Jubilee year is over. Did you know that their motto is: 'Millions now living will never die'? They mean themselves, but what if it turns out to be *everybody*?

"And that's only the beginning. Think of what the insurance companies are going to say. And what's going to happen to the whole structure of compound interest. Wells's old yarn about the man who lived so long that his savings came to dominate the world's whole financial structure—*When the Sleeper Wakes*, wasn't it?—well, that's going to be theoretically possible for *everybody* with the patience and the capital to let his money sit still. Or think of the whole corpus of the inheritance laws. It's going to be the biggest, blackest social explosion the West ever had to take. We'll be much too busy digging in to care about what's happening to the Central Committee in Moscow."

"You seem to care enough to be protecting the Central Committee's interests, or at least what they probably think of as their interests," Paige said slowly. "After all, there is a possibility of keeping the secret, instead of letting it leak."

"There is no such possibility," Anne said. "Natural laws can't be kept secret. Once you give a scientist the idea that a certain goal can be reached, you've given him more than half of the information he needs. Once he gets the idea that the conquest of death is possible, no power on Earth can stop him from finding out how it's done—the 'know-how' we make so many fatuous noises about is the most minor part of research, it's even a matter of total indifference to the essence of the question."

"I don't see that."

"Then let's go back to the fission bomb again for a moment. The only way we could have kept that a secret was to have failed to drop it at all, or even test-fire it. Once the secret was out that the bomb existed—and you'll remember that we announced that before hundreds of thousands of people in Hiroshima—we had no secrets in that field worth protecting. The biggest mystery in the Smyth report was the specific method by which uranium slugs were 'canned' in a protective jacket; it was one of the toughest problems the project had to lick, but at the same time it's exactly the kind of problem you'd assign to an engineer, and confidently expect a solution inside of a year.

"The fact of the matter, Paige, is that you can't keep scientific matters a secret from the other guy without keeping them a secret from yourself. A scientific secret is something that some other scientist can't *contribute to*, any more than he can profit by it. Contrariwise, if you arm yourself through discoveries in natural law, you also arm the other guy. Either you give him the information, or you cut your own throat; there aren't any other courses possible.

"And let me ask you this, Paige: should we give the USSR the advantage—temporary though it'll be—of having to get along *without* the anti-agathics for a while? By their very nature, the drugs will do more damage to the West than they will to the USSR. After all, in the Soviet Union one isn't permitted to inherit money, or to exercise any real control over economic forces just because one's lived a long time. If both major powers are given control over death at the same time, the West will be at a natural disadvantage. If we give control over death to the West alone, we'll be sabotaging our own civilization without putting the USSR under any comparable handicap. Is that sensible?"

The picture was staggering, to say the least. It gave Paige an impression of Gunn decidedly at variance with the mask of salesman-turned-executive which the man himself wore. But it was otherwise self-consistent; that, he knew, was supposed to be enough for him.

"How could I tell?" he said coldly. "All I can see is that every day I stick with you, I get in deeper. First I pose for the FBI as something that I'm not. Next I'm given possession of information that it's unlawful for me to have. And now I'm helping you two conceal the evidence of a high crime. It looks more and more to me as though I was supposed to be involved in this thing from the beginning. I don't see how you could have done so thorough a job on me without planning it."

"You needn't deny that you asked for it, Paige."

"I don't deny that," he said. "You don't deny deliberately involving me, either, I notice."

"No. It was deliberate, all right. I thought you'd have suspected it before. And if you're planning to ask me why, save your breath. I'm not permitted to tell you. You'll find out in due course."

"You two——"

"No. Tru had nothing to do with involving you. That was my idea. He only agreed to it—and he had to be convinced from considerably higher up."

"You two," Paige said through almost motionless lips, "don't hesitate to trample on the bystanders, do you? If I didn't know before that Pfitzner was run by a pack of idealists, I'd know it now. You've got the characteristic ruthlessness."

"That," Anne said in a level voice, "is what it takes."

8

Instead of sleeping after his trick—for now Helmuth knew that he was really afraid—he sat up in the reading chair in his cabin. The illuminated microfilmed pages of a book flicked by across the surface of the wall opposite him, timed precisely to the reading rate most comfortable for him, and he had several weeks' worry-conserved alcohol and smoke rations for ready consumption.

But Helmuth let his mix go flat, and did not notice the book, which had turned itself on, at the page where he had abandoned it last, when he had fitted himself into the chair. Instead, he listened to the radio.

There was always a great deal of ham radio activity in the Jovian system. The conditions were good for it, since there was plenty of power available, few impeding atmosphere layers and those thin, no Heaviside layers, and few official and no commercial channels with which the hams could interfere.

And there were plenty of people scattered about the satellites who needed the sound of a voice.

". . . anybody know whether or not the senators are coming here? Doc Barth put in a report a while back on a fossil plant he found here, at least he thinks it was a plant. Maybe they'd like a look at it."

"It's the Bridge team they're coming to see." A strong voice, and the impression of a strong transmitter wavering in and out to the currents of an atmosphere; that would be Sweeney, on Ganymede. "Sorry to throw the wet blanket, boys, but I don't think the senators'll be interested in our rock-balls for their own lumpy selves. They're only scheduled to stay here three days."

Helmuth thought greyly: *Then they'll stay on Callisto only one.*

"Is that you, Sweeney? Where's the Bridge tonight?"

"Dillon's on duty," a very distant transmitter said. "Try to raise Helmuth, Sweeney."

"Helmuth, Helmuth, you gloomy beetle-gooser! Come in, Helmuth!"

"Sure, Bob, come in and dampen us a little. We're feeling cheerful."

Sluggishly, Helmuth reached out to take the mike, from where it lay clipped to one arm of the chair. But before he had completed the gesture, the door to his room swung open.

Eva came in.

She said: "Bob, I want to tell you something."

"His voice is changing!" the voice of the Callisto operator said. "Sweeney, ask him what he's drinking!"

Helmuth cut the radio out. The girl was freshly dressed—in so far as anybody dressed in anything on Jupiter V—and Helmuth wondered why she was prowling the decks at this hour, half-way between her sleep period and her trick. Her hair was hazy against the light from the corridor, and she looked less mannish than usual. She reminded him a little of the way she had looked when they had first met, before the Bridge had come to bestride his bed instead. He put the memory aside.

"All right," he said. "I owe you a mix, I guess. Citric, sugar and the other stuff are in the locker . . . you know where it is. Shot-cans are there, too."

124

The girl shut the door and sat down on the bunk, with a free litheness that was almost grace, but with a determination which, Helmuth knew, meant that she had just decided to do something silly for all the right reasons.

"I don't need a drink," she said. "As a matter of fact, I've been turning my lux-R's back to the common pool. I suppose you did that for me—by showing me what a mind looks like that's hiding from itself."

"Evita, stop sounding like a tract. Obviously you've advanced to a higher, more Jovian plane of existence, but won't you still need your metabolism? Or have you decided that vitamins are all-in-the-mind?"

"Now you're being superior. Anyhow, alcohol isn't a vitamin. And I didn't come to talk about that. I came to tell you something I think you ought to know."

"Which is——?"

She said: "Bob, I mean to have a child here."

A bark of laughter, part sheer hysteria and part exasperation, jack-knifed Helmuth into a sitting position. A red arrow bloomed on the far wall, obediently marking the paragraph which, supposedly, he had reached in his reading. Eva twisted to look at it, but the page was already dimming and vanishing.

"Women!" Helmuth said, when he could get his breath back. "Really, Evita, you make me feel much better. No environment can change a human being much, after all."

"Why should it?" she said suspiciously, looking back at him. "I don't see the joke. Shouldn't a woman want to have a child?"

"Of course she should," he said, settling back. The pages began to flip across the wall again. "It's quite ordinary. All women want to have children. All women dream of the day they can turn a child out to play in an airless rock-garden like Jupiter V, to pluck fossils and make dust-castles and get quaintly star-burned. How cosy to tuck the blue little body back into its corner that night, and give it its oxygen bottle, promptly at the sound of the trick-change bell! Why, it's as natural as Jupiter-light—as Western as freeze-dried apple pie."

He turned his head casually away. "Congratulations. As for me, though, Eva, I'd much prefer that you take your ghostly little pretext out of here."

Eva surged to her feet in one furious motion. Her fingers grasped him by the beard and jerked his head painfully around again.

"You reedy male platitude!" she said, in a low grinding voice. "How you could see almost the whole point, and make so little of it—*Women*, is it? So you think I came creeping in here, full of humbleness, to settle our technical differences in bed!"

He closed his hand on her wrist and twisted it away. "What else?" he demanded, trying to imagine how it would feel to stay reasonable for five minutes at a time with these Bridge-robots. "None of us need bother with games and excuses. We're here, we're isolated, we were all chosen because, among other things, we were judged incapable of forming permanent emotional attachments, and capable of any alliances we liked—without going unbalanced when the attraction died and the alliance came unstuck. None of us have to pretend that our living arrangements would keep us out of jail in Boston, or that they have to involve any Earth-normal excuses."

She said nothing. After a while he asked, gently: "Isn't that so?"

"Of course it's not so," Eva said. She was frowning at him; he had the absurd impression that she was pity-

126

ing him. "If we were really incapable of making any permanent attachment, we'd never have been chosen. A cast of mind like that is a mental disease, Bob; it's anti-survival from the ground up. It's the conditioning that made us this way. Didn't you know?"

Helmuth hadn't known; or if he had, he had been conditioned to forget it. He gripped the arms of the chair tighter.

"Anyhow," he said, "that's the way we are."

"Yes, it is. Also it has nothing to do with the matter."

"It doesn't? How stupid do you think I am? *I* don't care whether or not you've decided to have a child here, if you really mean what you say."

She, too, seemed to be trembling. "You really don't, too. The decision means nothing to you."

"Well, if I liked children, I'd be sorry for the child. But as it happens, I can't stand children—and if that's the conditioning, too, I can't do a thing about it. In short, Eva, as far as I'm concerned you can have as many kids as you want, and to me you'll *still* be the worst operator on the Bridge."

"I'll bear that in mind," she said. At this moment she seemed to have been cut from pressure-ice. "I'll leave you something to charge your mind with, too, Robert Helmuth. I'll leave you sprawled here under your precious book . . . what is Madame Bovary to you, anyhow, you unadventurous turtle? . . . to think about a man who believes that children must always be born into warm cradles—a man who thinks that men have to huddle on warm worlds, or they won't survive. A man with no ears, no eyes, scarcely any head. A man in terror, a man crying: Mamma! *Mamma!* all the stellar days and nights long!"

"Parlour diagnosis."

127

"Parlour labelling! Good trick, Bob. Draw your warm woolly blanket in tight around your brains, or some little sneeze of sense might creep in, and impair your—efficiency!"

The door closed sharply after her.

A million pounds of fatigue crashed down without warning on the back of Helmuth's neck, and he fell back into the reading chair with a gasp. The roots of his beard ached, and Jupiters bloomed and wavered away before his closed eyes.

He struggled once, and fell asleep.

Instantly he was in the grip of the dream.

It started, as always, with commonplaces, almost realistic enough to be a documentary film-strip—except for the appalling sense of pressure, and the distorted emotional significance with which the least word, the smallest movement was invested.

It was the sinking of the first caisson of the Bridge. The actual event had been bad enough. The job demanded enough exactness of placement to require that manned ships enter Jupiter's atmosphere itself: a squadron of twenty of the most powerful ships ever built, with the five-million-ton asteroid, trimmed and shaped in space, slung beneath them in an immense cat's-cradle.

Four times that squadron had disappeared beneath the racing clouds; four times the tense voices of pilots and engineers had muttered in Helmuth's ears, and he had whispered back, trying to guide them by what he could see of the conflicting trade-blasts from Jupiter V; four times there were shouts and futile orders and the snapping of cables and men screaming endlessly against the eternal howl of the Jovian sky.

It had cost, altogether, nine ships, and two hundred

thirty-one men, to get one of five laboriously-shaped asteroids planted in the shifting slush that was Jupiter's surface. Until that had been accomplished, the Bridge could never have been more than a dream. While the Great Red Spot had shown astronomers that some structures on Jupiter could last for long periods of time —long enough, at least, to be seen by many generations of human beings—it had been equally well known that nothing on Jupiter could be really permanent. The planet did not even have a "surface" in the usual sense; instead, the bottom of the atmosphere merged more or less smoothly into a high-pressure sludge, which in turn thickened as it went deeper into solid pressure-ice. At no point on the way down was there any interface between one layer and another, except in the rare areas where a part of the deeper, more "solid" medium had been thrust far up out of its normal level, to form a continent which might last as long as two years, or two hundred. It was on to one of these great ribs of bulging ice that the ships had tried to plant their asteroid—and, after four tries, had succeeded.

Helmuth had helped to supervise all five operations, counting the successful one, from his desk on Jupiter V. But in the dream he was not in the control shack, but instead on shipboard, in one of the ships that was never to come back——

Then, without transition, but without any sense of discontinuity either, he was on the Bridge itself. Not *in absentia*, as the remote guiding intelligence of a beetle, but in person, in an ovular, tank-like suit the details of which would never come clear. The high brass had discovered antigravity, and had asked for volunteers to man the Bridge. Helmuth had volunteered.

Looking back on it, in the dream, he did not understand why he had volunteered. It had simply seemed expected of him, and he had not been able to help it, even though he had known to begin with what it would be like. He belonged on the Bridge, though he hated it —he had been doomed to go there, from the first.

And there was . . . something wrong . . . with the antigravity. The high brass had asked for its volunteers before the research work had been completed. The present antigravity fields were weak, and there was some basic flaw in the theory. Generators broke down after only short periods of use; burned out, unpredictably, sometimes only moments after having passed their production tests with perfect scores. In waking life, vacuum tubes behaved in that unpredictable way; there were no vacuum tubes anywhere on Jupiter, but machines on Jupiter burned out all the same, burned out at temperatures which would freeze Helmuth solid in an instant.

That was what Helmuth's antigravity set was about to do. He crouched inside his personal womb, above the boiling sea, the clouds raging by him in little scouring crystals which wore at the chorion protecting him, lit by a plume of hydrogen flame—and waited to feel his weight suddenly become three times greater than normal, the pressure on his body go from sixteen pounds per square inch to fifteen million, the air around him take on the searing stink of poisons, the whole of Jupiter come pressing its burden upon him.

He knew what would happen to him then.

It happened.

Helmuth greeted "morning" on Jupiter V with his customary scream.

BOOK THREE

*

ENTR'ACTE

4th January 2020

Dear Seppi,

Lord knows I have better sense than to mail this, send it to you by messenger, or leave it anywhere in the files—or indeed on the premises—of the Joint Committee; but if one is sensible about such matters these days, one never puts anything on paper at all, and then burns the carbons. As a bad compromise, I am filing this among my personal papers, where it will be found, opened and sent to you only after I will be beyond reprisals.

That's not meant to sound as ominous as, upon re-reading, I see it does. By the time you have this letter, abundant details of what I've been up to should be available to you, not only through the usual press garble, but through verbatim testimony. You will have worked out, by now, a rational explanation of my conduct since my re-election (and before it, for that matter). At the very least, I hope you now know why I authorized such a monstrosity as the Bridge, even against your very good advice.

All that is water over the dam (or ether over the Bridge, if you boys are following Dirac's lead back to the ether these days. How do I know about that? You'll see in a moment.) I don't mean to rehash it here. What I want to do in this letter is to leave you a more specialized memo, telling you in detail just how well the research system you suggested to me worked out for us.

Despite my surface appearance of ignoring that advice, we were following your suggestion, and very closely. I took a particular interest in your hunch that there might be "crackpot" ideas on gravity which needed investigation. Frankly, I had no hope of finding anything, but that would have left me no worse off than I had been before I talked to you. And actually it wasn't very long before my research chief came up with the Locke Derivation.

The research papers which finally emerged from this particular investigation are still in the Graveyard file, and I have no hope that they'll be released to non-government physicists within the foreseeable future. If you don't get the story from me, you'll never get it from anyone; and I've enough on my conscience now to be indifferent to a small crime like breaking Security. Besides, as usual, this particular "secret" has been available for the taking for years. A man named Schuster—you may know more about him than I do—wondered out loud about it as far back as 1891, before anybody had thought of trying to keep scientific matters a secret. He wanted to know whether or not every large rotating mass, like the Sun for instance, was a natural magnet. (That was before the sun's magnetic field had been discovered, too.) And by the 1940s it was clearly established for *small* rotating bodies like electrons—a thing called the Lande factor with which I'm sure you're familiar. I myself don't understand Word One of it. (Dirac was associated with much of that part of the work.) Finally, a man named W. H. Babcock, of Mount Wilson, pointed out in the 1940s that the Lande factor for the Earth, the Sun, and a star named 78 Virginius was identical, or damned close to it.

Now all this seemed to me to have nothing to do at all with gravity, and I said so to my team chief, who brought the thing to my attention. But I was wrong (I suppose you're already ahead of me by now). Another man, Prof. P. M. S. Blackett, whose name was even familiar to *me*, had pointed out the relationship. Suppose, Blackett said (I am copying from my notes now), we let P be magnetic moment, or what I have to think of as the leverage effect of a magnet—the product of the strength of the charge times the distance between the poles. Let U be angular momentum—rotation to a slob like me; angular speed times moment of inertia to you. Then if C is the velocity of light, and G is the acceleration of gravity (and they always are in equations like this, I'm told), then:

$$P = \frac{BG\frac{1}{2}U}{2C}$$

(B is supposed to be a constant amounting to about 0·25. Don't ask me why.) Admittedly this was all speculative; there would be no way to test it, except on another planet with a stronger magnetic field than Earth's—preferably about a hundred times as strong. The closest we could come to that would be Jupiter, where the speed of rotation is about 25,000 miles an hour at the equator—and that was obviously out of the question.

Or was it? I confess that I never thought of using Jupiter, except in wish-fulfilment daydreams, until this matter of the Locke Derivation came up. It seems that by a simple algebraic manipulation, you can stick G on one side of the equation, and all the other terms on the other, and come up with this:

$$G=\left(\frac{2PC}{BU}\right)^2$$

To test that, you need a gravitational field little more than twice the strength of Earth's. And there, of course, is Jupiter again. None of my experts would give the notion a nickel—they said, among other things, that nobody even knew who Locke was, which is true, and that his algebraic trick wouldn't stand up under dimensional analysis, which turned out to be also true—but irrelevant. (We *did* have to monkey with it a little after the experimental results were in.) What counted was that we could make a practical use of this relationship.

Once we tried that, I should add, we were astonished at the accompanying effects: the abolition of the Lorentz-Fitzgerald relationship inside the field, the intolerance of the field itself to matter outside its influence, and so on; not only at their occurring at all—the formula doesn't predict them—but at their order of magnitude. I'm told that when this thing gets out, dimensional analysis isn't the only scholium that's going to have to be revamped. It's going to be the greatest headache for physicists since the Einstein theory; I don't know whether you'll relish this premonitory twinge or not.

Pretty good going for a "crackpot" notion, though.

After that, the Bridge was inevitable. As soon as it became clear that we could perform the necessary tests only on the surface of Jupiter itself, we had to have the Bridge. It also became clear that the Bridge would have to be a dynamic structure. It couldn't be built to a certain size and stopped there. The moment it was stopped, Jupiter would tear it to shreds. We had to build it to grow—to do more than just resist Jupiter—to push back against Jupiter, instead. It's double the size that it needed to be to test the Locke Derivation, now, and I still don't know how much longer we're going to have to keep it growing. Not long, I hope; the thing's a monster already.

But Seppi, let me ask you this: Does the Bridge really fall under the interdict you uttered against gigantic research projects? It's gigantic, all right. But—is it gigantic *on Jupiter*? I say it isn't. It's peanuts. A piece of attic gadgetry and nothing more. And we couldn't have performed the necessary experiments on any other planet.

Not all the wealth of Ormus or of Ind, or of all the world down all the ages, could have paid for a Manhattan District scaled to Jupiter's size.

In addition—though this was incidental—the apparent giganticism involved was a useful piece of misdirection. Elephantine research projects may be just about played out, but government budgetry agencies are used to them and think them normal. Getting the Joint Committee involved in one helped to revive the committeemen from their comatose state, as nothing else could have. It got us appropriations we never could have corralled otherwise, because people associate such projects with weapons research. And—forgive me, but there is a sort of science to politics too—it seemed to show graphically that I was *not* following the suspect advice of the suspect, Dr. Corsi. I owed you that, though it's hardly as large a payment as I would like to make.

But I don't mean to talk about the politics of crackpot-mining here; only about the concrete results. You should be warned, too, that the method has its pitfalls.

You will know by now about the anti-agathic research, and what we got out of it. I talked to people who might know what the chances were, and got general agreement from them as to how we should proceed. This straight-line approach looked good to me from the beginning —I set the Pfitzner people to work on it at once, since they already had that HWS appropriation for similar research, and HWS wouldn't be alert enough to detect the moment when Pfitzner's target changed from just plain old age to death itself. But we didn't overlook the crackpots—and before long we found a real dilly.

This was a man named Lyons, who insisted that the standard Lansing hypothesis, which postulates the existence of an ageing-toxin, was exactly the opposite of the truth. (I go into this subject with a certain relish, because I suspect that you know as little about it as I do; it's not often that I find myself in that situation.) Instead, he said, what happens is that it's the *young* mothers who pass on to their offspring some substance which makes them long-lived. Lansing's notion that the old mothers were the ones who did the passing along, and that the substance passed along speeding up age-ing, was unproven, Lyons said.

Well, that threw us into something of a spiral. Lansing's Law—"Senescence begins when growth ends"— had been regarded as gospel in gerontology for decades. But Lyons had a good hypothetical case. He pointed out that, among other things, all of Lansing's long-lived rotifers showed characteristics in common with polyploid individuals. In addition to being hardy and long-lived, they were of unusually large size, and they were less fertile than normal rotifers. Suppose that the substance which was passed along from one generation to another was a chromosome-doubler, like colchicine?

We put that question to Lansing's only surviving student, a living crotchet named MacDougal. He wouldn't hear of it; to him it was like questioning the Word of God. Besides, he said, if Lyons is right, how do you propose to test it? Rotifers are microscopic animals. Except for their eggs, their body-cells are invisible even under the microscope. It would be quite a few months of Sundays before we ever got a look at a rotifer chromosome.

Lyons thought he had an answer for that. He proposed to develop a technique of microtome preparation which would make, not one, but several different slices through a rotifer's egg. With any sort of luck, he said, we might be able to extend the technique to rotifer spores, and maybe even to the adult critters.

We thought we ought to try it. Without telling Pfitzner about it, we gave Pearl River Labs that headache. We put Lyons himself in charge, and assigned Mac-Dougal to act as a consultant (which he did by sniping and scoffing every minute of the day, until not only Lyons, but everybody else in the plant hated him). It was awful. Rotifers, it turns out, are incredibly delicate animals, just about impossible to preserve after they're dead, no matter what stage of their development you catch them in. Time and time again, Lyons came up with microscope slides which, he said, *proved* that the long-lived rotifers were at least triploid—three labelled chromosomes per body-cell instead of two—and maybe even tetraploid. Every other expert in the Pearl River plant looked at them, and saw nothing but a blur which might have been rotifer chromosomes, and might equally well have been a newspaper halftone of a grey cat walking over a fur rug in a thick fog. The comparative tests—producing polyploid rotifers and other critters with drugs like colchicine, and comparing them with the critters produced by Lansing's and Mac-Dougal's classical breeding methods—were just as indecisive. Lyons finally decided that what he needed to prove his case was the world's biggest and most expensive X-ray microscope, and right then we shut him down.

MacDougal had been right all the time. Lyons was a crackpot with a plausible line of chatter, enough of a technique at microdissection to compel respect, and a real and commendable eagerness to explore his idea right down to the bottom. MacDougal was a frozen-brained old man with far too much reverence for his teacher, a man far too ready to say that a respected notion was right because it was respected, and a man who had performed no actual experiments himself since his student days. But he had been right—purely intuitively—in predicting that Lyons' inversion of Lansing's Law would come to nothing. I gather that victory in the sciences doesn't always go to the most personable man, any more than it does in any other field. I'm glad to know it; I'm always glad to find some small area of human endeavour which resists the con-man and the sales-talk.

When Pfitzner discovered ascomycin, we had HWS close Pearl River out entirely.

Negative results of this kind are valuable for scientists too, I'm told. How you will evaluate your proposed research method in the light of these two experiences is unknown to me; I can only tell you what I think *I* learned. I am convinced that we must be much slower, in the future, to ignore the fringe notion and the marginal theorist. One of the virtues of these crackpots—if that is what they are—is that they tend to cling to ideas which can be tested. That's worth hanging on to, in a world where scientific ideas have become so abstract that even their originators can't suggest ways to test them. Whoever Locke was, I suppose he hadn't put a thousandth as much time into thinking about gravity as Blackett had; yet Blackett couldn't suggest a way to test his equation, whereas the Locke Derivation was testable (on Jupiter) and turned out to be right. As for Lyons, his notion was wrong; but it too fell down because it failed the operational test, the very test it proposed to pass; until we performed that test, we had no real assessment of Lansing's Law, which had been travelling for years on prestige because of the "impossibility" of weighing any contrary hypothesis. Lyons forced us to do that, and enlarged our knowledge.

And so, take it from there; I've tried to give back as good as I have gotten. I'm not going to discuss the politics of this whole conspiracy with you, nor do I want you to concern yourself with them. Politics is death. Above all, I beg you—if you're at all pleased with this report—not to be distressed over the situation I will probably be in by the time this reaches you. I've been ruthless with your reputation to advance my purposes; I've been ruthless with the careers of some other people; I've been quite ruthless in sending some men—some hundreds of men—to deaths they could surely have avoided had it not been for me; I've put many others, including a number of children, into considerable jeopardy. With all this written against my name, I'd think it a monstrous injustice to get off scot-free.

And that is all I can say; I have an appointment in a few minutes. Thank you for your friendship and your help.

BLISS WAGONER

★
★ 9 ★

Ruthlessness, Anne had said, is what it takes. But—Paige thought afterwards—is it?

Does faith add up to its own flat violation? It was all well enough to have something in which you could believe. But when a faith in humanity-in-general automatically results in casual inhumanity toward individual people, something must have gone awry. Should the temple bell be struck so continually that it has to shatter, and make all its worshippers ill with terror until it is silenced?

Silence. The usual answer. Or was the fault not in faith itself, but in the faithful? The faithful were usually pretty frightening as people, Witnesses and humanitarians alike.

Paige's time to debate the point with himself had already almost run out—and with it, his time to protect himself, if he could. Nothing had emerged from his soil samples. Evidently bacterial life on the Jovian moons had never at any time been profuse, and consisted now only of a few hardy spores of common species, like *Bacillus subtilis*, which occurred on every Earth-like world and sometimes even in meteors. The samples plated out sparsely and yielded nothing which had not been known for decades—as, indeed, the statistics of this kind of research had predicted from the beginning.

It was now known around the Bronx plant that some sort of investigation of the Pfitzner project was rolling, and was already moving too fast to be derailed by any method the company's executives could work out. Daily reports from Pfitzner's Washington office—actually the Washington branch of Interplanet Press, the public relations agency Pfitzner maintained—were filed in the plant, but they were apparently not very informative. Paige gathered that there was some mystery about the investigation at the source, though neither Gunn nor Anne would say so in so many words.

And, finally, Paige's leave was to be over, day after tomorrow. After that, the Proserpine station—and probably an order to follow, emerging out of the investigation, which would maroon him there for the rest of his life in the service.

And it wasn't worth it.

That realization had been staring him in the eyes all along. For Anne and Gunn, perhaps, the price was worth paying, the tricks were worth playing, the lying and the cheating and the risking of the lives of others were necessary and just to the end in view. But when the last card was down, Paige knew that he himself lacked the necessary dedication. Like every other road toward dedication that he had assayed, this one had turned out to have been paved with pure lead—and had left him with no better emblem of conduct than the miserable one which had kept him going all the same: self-preservation.

He knew then, with cold disgust toward himself, that he was going to use what he knew to clear himself, as soon as the investigation hit the plant. Senator Wagoner, the grapevine said, would be conducting it—oddly enough, for Wagoner and MacHinery were deadly political enemies; had MacHinery gotten the jump on him at last?—and would arrive tomorrow. If Paige timed himself very carefully, he could lay down the facts, leave the plant for ever, and be out in space without having to face Tru Gunn or Anne Abbott at all. What would happen to the Pfitzner project thereafter would be old news by the time he landed at the Proserpine station—more than three months old.

And by that time, he told himself, he would no longer care.

Nevertheless, when the quick morrow came, he marched in to Gunn's office—which Wagoner had taken over—like a man going before a firing squad.

A moment later, he felt as though he had been shot down while still crossing the door-sill. Even before he realized that Anne was already in the room, he heard Wagoner say:

"Colonel Russell, sit down. I'm glad to see you. I have a security clearance for you, and a new set of orders; you can forget Proserpine. You and Miss Abbott and I are leaving for Jupiter. Tonight."

It was like a dream after that. In the Caddy on the way to the spaceport, Wagoner said nothing. As for Anne, she seemed to be in a state of slight shock. From what little Paige thought he had learned about her— and it was very little—he deduced that she had expected this as little as he had. Her face as he had entered Gunn's office had been guarded, eager, and slightly smug all at once, as though she had thought she'd know what Wagoner would say. But when Wagoner had mentioned Jupiter, she'd turned to look at him as though he'd been turned from a senator into a boxing kangaroo, in the plain sight of the Pfitzner

144

Founders. Something was wrong. After the long cata-
logue of things already visibly wrong, the statement
didn't mean very much. But something had clearly gone
wrong.

There were fireworks in the sky to the south, visible
from the right side of the Caddy where Paige sat as the
car turned east on to the parkway. They were big and
spectacular, and seemed to be going up from the heart
of Manhattan. Paige was puzzled until he remembered, like a fact recalled from the heart of an absurd
dream, that this was the last night of the Witness Revival, being held in the stadium on Randalls Island.
The fireworks celebrated the Second Coming, which
the Witnesses were confident could not now be long
delayed.

> *Gewiss, gewiss, es naht noch heut'*
> *und kann nicht lang mehr säumen. . . .*

Paige could remember having heard his father, an
ardent Wagnerian, singing that; it was from *Tristan*.
But he thought instead of those frightening medieval
paintings of the Second Coming, in which Christ stands
ignored in a corner of the canvas while the people flock
reverently to the feet of the Anti-Christ, whose face, in
the dim composite of Paige's memory, was a curious
mixture of Francis X. MacHinery and Bliss Wagoner.

Words began to bloom along the black sky at the
hearts of starshells:

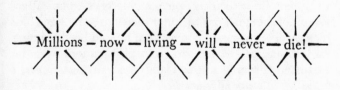

— Millions — now — living — will — never — die! —

No doubt, Paige thought bleakly. The Witnesses also believed that the Earth was flat; but Paige was on his way to Jupiter—not exactly a round planet, but rounder than the Witnesses' Earth. In quest, if you please, of immortality, in which he too had believed. Tasting bile, he thought, *It takes all kinds.*

A final starshell, so brilliant even at this distance that the word inside it was almost dazzled out, burst sound-lessly into blue-white fire above the city. It said:

Paige swung his head abruptly and looked at Anne. Her face, a ghostly blur in the dying light of the shell, was turned raptly toward the window; she had been watching, too. He leaned forward and kissed her slightly parted lips, gently, forgetting all about Wag-oner. After a frozen moment he could feel her mouth smiling against his, the smile which had astonished him so when he had seen it first, but softened, transformed, giving. The world went away for a while.

Then she touched his cheeks with her fingertips and sank back against the cushions; the Caddy swung sharply north off the parkway; and the spark of radi-ance which was the last retinal image of the shell vanished into drifting purple blotches, like after-visions of the sun—or of Jupiter seen close-on. Anne had no way of knowing, of course, that he had been running away from her, toward the Proserpine station, when he had been cornered in this Caddy instead. *Anne, Anne, I believe; help me in mine unbelief.*

The Caddy was passed through the spaceport gates after a brief, whispered consultation between the chauffeur and the guards. Instead of driving directly for the Administration Building, however, it turned craftily to the left and ran along the inside of the wire fence, back toward the city and into the dark reaches of the emergency landing pits. It was not totally dark there, however; there was a pool of light on an apron some distance ahead, with a needle of glare pointing straight up from its centre.

Paige leaned forward and peered through the double glass barrier—one pane between himself and the driver, the other between the driver and the world. The needle of light was a ship, but it was not one he recognized. It was a single-stage job: a ferry, then, designed to take them out no farther than to Satellite Vehicle One, where they would be transferred to a proper interplanetary vessel. But it was small, even for a ferry.

"How do you like her, Colonel?" Wagoner's voice said, unexpectedly, from the black corner where he sat.

"All right," Paige said. "She's a little small, isn't she?"

Wagoner chuckled. "Pretty damn small," he said, and fell silent again. Alarmed, Paige began to wonder if the senator was feeling entirely well. He turned to look at Anne, but he could not even see her face now. He groped for her hand; she responded with a feverish, rigid grip.

The Caddy shot abruptly away from the fence, with a smoothness and a silence that bespoke gasolene in the fuel tank, not kerosene. It bore down on the pool of light. Paige could see several marines standing on the apron at the tail of the ship. Absurdly, the vessel looked even smaller as it came closer.

"All right," Wagoner said. "Out of here, both of you. We'll be taking off in ten minutes. The crewmen will show you your quarters."

"Crewmen?" Paige said. "Senator, that ship won't hold more than four people, and one of them has to be the tube-man. That leaves nobody to pilot her but me."

"Not this trip," Wagoner said, following him out of the car. "We're only passengers, you and I and Miss Abbott, and of course the marines. The *Per Aspera* has a separate crew of five. Let's not waste time, please."

It was impossible. On the cleats, Paige felt as though he were trying to climb into a ·22 calibre long-rifle cartridge. To get ten people into this tiny shell, you'd have to turn them into some sort of human concentrate and pour them in, like powdered coffee.

Nevertheless, one of the marines met him in the airlock, and within another minute he was strapping himself down inside a windowless cabin as big as any he'd ever seen on board a standard interplanetary vessel—far bigger than any ferry could acccommodate. The intercom box at the head of his hammock was already calling the clearance routine.

"Dog down and make all fast. Airlock will cycle in one minute."

What had happened to Anne? She had come up the cleats after him, of that he was sure——

"All fast. Take-off in one minute. Passengers 'ware G's."

——but he'd been hustled down to this nonsensical cabin too fast to look back. There was something very wrong. Was Wagoner——

"Thirty seconds. 'Ware G's."

——making some sort of a getaway? Bur from what?

148

And why did he want to take Paige and Anne with
him? As hostages they were——

"Twenty seconds."

——worthless, since they were of no value to the
government, had no money, knew nothing damning
about Wagoner——

"Fifteen seconds."

But wait a minute. Anne knew something about
Wagoner, or thought she did.

"Ten seconds. Stand by."

The call made him relax instinctively. There would
be time to think about that later. At take-off——

"Five seconds."

——it didn't pay——

"Four."

——to concentrate——

"Three."

——on anything——

"Two."

——else but——

"One."

——actual——

"Zero."

——*take-off* hit him with the abrupt, bone-cracking,
gut-wrenching impact of all ferry take-offs. There was
nothing you could do to ameliorate it but let the strong
muscles of the arms and legs and back bear it as best
they could, with the automatic tetanus of the Seyle GA
reaction, and concentrate on keeping your head and
your abdomen in exact neutral with the acceleration
thrust. The muscles you used for that were seldom
called upon on the ground, even by weight-lifters, but
you learned to use them or were invalided out of the

service; a trained spaceman's abdominal muscles will bounce a heavy rock, and no strong man can make him turn his head if his neck muscles say *no*.

Also, it helped a little to yell. Theoretically, the yell collapses the lungs—acceleration pneumothorax, the books call it—and keeps them collapsed until the surge of powered flight is over. By that time, the carbon dioxide level of the blood has risen so high that the breathing reflex will reassert itself with an enormous gasp, even if crucial chest muscles have been torn. The yell makes sure that when next you breathe, you *breathe*.

But more importantly for Paige and every other spaceman, the yell was the only protest he could form against that murderous nine seconds of pressure; it makes you *feel* better. Paige yelled with vigour.

He was still yelling when the ship went into free fall.

Instantly, while the yell was still dying incredulously in his throat, he was clawing at his harness. All his spaceman's reflexes had gone off at once. The powered-flight period had been too short. Even the shortest possible take-off acceleration outlasts the yell. Yet the ion-rockets were obviously silenced. The little ship's power had failed—she was falling back to Earth——

"Attention, please," the intercom box said mildly. "We are now under way. Free fall will last only a few seconds. Stand by for restoration of normal gravity."

And then. . . . And then the hammock against which Paige was struggling was *down* again, as though the ship were still resting quietly on Earth. Impossible; she couldn't even be out of the atmosphere yet. Even if she were, free fall should last all the rest of the trip. Gravity in an interplanetary vessel—let alone a ferry—could be re-established only by rotating the ship around its long axis; few captains bothered with the fuel-expensive manœuvre, since hardly anybody but old hands flew between the planets. Besides, this ship—the *Per Aspera*—hadn't gone through any such manœuvre, or Paige would have detected it.

Yet his body continued to press down against the hammock with an acceleration of one Earth gravity.

"Attention, please. We will be passing the Moon in one point two minutes. The observation blister is now open to passengers. Senator Wagoner requests the presence of Miss Abbott and Colonel Russell in the blister."

There was no further sound from the ion-rockets, which had inexplicably been shut off when the *Per Aspera* could have been no more than 250 miles above the surface of the Earth. Yet she was passing the Moon now, without the slightest sensation of movement, though she must still be accelerating. What was driving her? Paige could hear nothing but the small hum of the ship's electrical generator, no louder than it would have been on the ground, unburdened of the job of RF-heating the electron-ion plasma which the rockets used. Grimly, he unsnapped the last gripper from his harness, conscious of what a baby he evidently was on board this ship, and got up.

The deck felt solid and abnormal under his feet, pressing against the soles of his shoes with a smug terrestrial pressure of one unvarying gravity. Only the habits of caution of a service lifetime prevented him from running forward up the companionway to the observation blister.

Anne and Senator Wagoner were there, the dimming moonlight bathing their backs as they looked ahead into deep space. Shining between them was a brilliant, hard spot of yellow-white light, glaring into the blister through the thick, cosmics-proof glass. The spot was fixed and steady, as were all the stars looking into the blister; proof positive that the ship's gravity was not being produced by axial spin. The yellow spot itself, shining between Wagoner's elbow and Anne's upper arm, was——

Jupiter.

On either side of the planet were two smaller bright dots: the four Galilean satellites, as widely separated to Paige's naked eye as they would have looked on Earth through a telescope the size of Galileo's.

While Paige hesitated in the doorway to the blister, the little spots that were Jupiter's largest moons visibly drew apart from each other a little, until one of them went into occultation behind Anne's right shoulder. The *Per Aspera* was still accelerating; it was driving toward Jupiter at a speed nothing in Paige's experience could have prepared him for. Stunned, he made a very rough estimate in his head of the increase in parallax and tried to calculate the ship's rate of approach from that.

The little lunar ferry, humming scarcely louder than a transformer for a model railroad system, obviously incapable of carrying five people—let alone ten—as far as SV-1, was now hurtling toward Jupiter at about a quarter of the speed of light.

At least forty thousand miles per second.

And the deepening colour of Jupiter showed that the *Per Aspera* was still picking up speed.

"Come in, Colonel Russell," Wagoner's voice said, echoing slightly in the blister. "Come watch the show. We've been waiting for you."

★ 10 ★

The ship that landed as Helmuth was going on duty did nothing to lighten the load on his heart. In shape it was not distinguishable from any of the short-range ferries which covered the Jovian satellary circuit, carrying supplies from the regular SV-1-Mars-Belt-Jupiter X cruiser to the inner moons—and, sometimes, some years-old mail; but it was considerably bigger than the usual Jovian ferry, and it grounded its outsize mass on Jupiter V with only the briefest cough of rockets.

That landing told Helmuth that his dream was well on its way to coming true. If the high brass had a real antigravity, there would have been no reason why the ion-streams should have been necessary at all. Obviously, what had been discovered was some sort of partial gravity screen, which allowed a ship to operate with far less rocket thrust than was usual, but which still left it subject to a sizeable fraction of the universal G, the inherent stress of space.

Nothing less than a complete, and completely controllable gravity screen would do, on Jupiter.

And theory said that a complete gravity screen was impossible. Once you set one up—even supposing that you could—you would be unable to enter it or leave it. Crossing a boundary-line between a one G field and a

153

no-G field would be precisely as difficult as surmounting a high-jump with the bar set at infinity, and for the same reasons. If you crossed it from the other direction, you would hit the ground on the other side of the line as hard as though you had fallen there from the Moon; a little harder, in fact.

Helmuth worked mechanically at the gang board, thinking. Charity was not in evidence, but there was no special reason why the foreman's board had to be manned on this trick. The work could be as easily supervised from here, and obviously Charity had expected Helmuth to do it that way, or he would have left notice. Probably Charity was already conferring with the senators, receiving what would be for him the glad news.

Helmuth realized suddenly that there was nothing left for him to do now, once this trick was over, but to cut and run.

There could be no real reason why he should be required to re-enact the entire nightmare, helplessly, event for event, like an actor committed to a role. He was awake now, in full control of his own senses, and still at least partially sane. The man in the dream had volunteered—but that man would not be Robert Helmuth. Not any longer.

While the senators were here on Jupiter V, he would turn in his resignation. Direct—over Charity's head.

The wave of relief came washing over him just as he finished resetting the circuits which would enable him to supervise from the gang board, and left him so startlingly weak that he had to put the helmet down on the ledge before he had raised it half-way to his head. So *that* had been what he had been waiting for: to quit, nothing more.

154

He owed it to Charity to finish the Grand Tour of the Bridge. After that, he'd be free. He would never have to see the Bridge again, not even inside a viewing helmet. A farewell tour, and then back to Chicago, if there was still such a place.

He waited until his breathing had quieted a little, scooped the helmet up on to his shoulders, and the Bridge . . .

. . . came falling into existence all around him, a Pandemonium beyond broaching and beyond hope, sealed on all sides. The drumfire of rain against his beetle's hull was so loud that it hurt his ears, even with the gain knob of his helmet backed all the way down to the thumb-stop. It was impossible to cut the audio circuit out altogether; much of his assessment of how the Bridge was responding to stress depended on sound; human eyesight on the Bridge was almost as useless as a snail's.

And the Bridge was responding now, as always, with its medley of dissonance and cacophony: *crang . . . crang . . . spungg . . . skreek . . . crang . . . ungg . . . oingg . . . skreek . . . skreek. . . .* These structural noises were the only ones that counted; they were the polyphony of the Bridge, everything else was decorative and to be ignored by the Bridge operator—the fioritura shrieking of the winds, the battery of the rain, the pedal diapason of thunder, the distant grumbling roll of the stage-hand volcanoes pushing continents back and forth on castors down below.

This time, however, at long last, it was impossible to ignore any part of this great orchestra. Its composite uproar was enormous, implacable, incredible even for Jupiter, overwhelming even in this season. The moment he heard it, Helmuth knew that he had waited too long.

The Bridge was not going to last much longer. Not unless every man and woman on Jupiter V fought without sleep to keep it up, throughout this passage of the Red Spot and the South Tropical Disturbance——

——if even that would serve. The great groans that were rising through the tornado-riven mists from the caissons were becoming steadily, spasmodically deeper; their hinges were already overloaded. And the deck of the Bridge was beginning to rise and fall a little, as though slow, frozen waves were passing along it from one unfinished end to the other. The queasy, lazy tidal swell made the beetle tip first its nose into the winds, then its tail, then back again, so that it took almost all of the current Helmuth could feed into the magnet windings to keep the craft stuck to the rails on the deck at all. Cruising the deck seemed to be out of the question; there was not enough power left over for the engines—almost every available erg had to be devoted to staying put.

But there was still the rest of the Grand Tour to be made. And still one direction which Helmuth had yet to explore:

Straight down.

Down to the ice; down to the Ninth Circle, where everything stops, and never starts again.

There was a set of tracks leading down one of the Bridge's great buttresses, on to which Helmuth could switch the beetle in nearby sector 94. It took him only a few moments to set the small craft to creeping head downward toward the surface.

The meters on the ghost board had already told him that the wind velocity fell off abruptly at twenty-one miles—that is, eleven miles down from the deck—in this sector, which was in the lee of The Glacier, a long rib of mountain-range which terminated near by. He was unprepared, however, for the near-calm itself. There was some wind, of course, as there was everywhere on Jupiter, especially at this season; but the worst gusts were little more than a few hundred miles per hour, and occasionally the meter fell as low as seventy-five.

The lull was dream-like. The beetle crawled downward through it, like a skin-diver who has already passed the safety-knot on his line, but is too drugged by the ecstasy of the depths to care. At fifteen miles, something white flashed in the fan-lights, and was gone. Then another; three more. And then, suddenly, a whole stream of them.

Belatedly, Helmuth stopped the beetle and peered ahead, but the white things were gone now. No, there were more of them, drifting quite slowly through the lights. As the wind died momentarily, they almost seemed to hover, pulsating slowly——

Helmuth heard himself grunt with astonishment. Once, in a moment of fancy, he had thought of Jovian jellyfish. That was what these looked like—jellyfish, not of the sea, but of the air. They were ten-ribbed, translucent, ranging in size from that of a closed fist to one as big as a football. They were beautiful—and looked incredibly delicate for this furious planet.

Helmuth reached forward to turn up the lights, but the wind rose just as his hand closed on the knob, and the creatures were gone. In the increased glare, Helmuth saw instead that there was a large platform jutting out from the buttress not far below him, just to one side of the rails. It was enclosed and roofed, but the material was transparent. And there was motion inside it.

He had no idea what the structure could be; evidently it was recent. Although he had never been below the deck in this sector before, he knew the plans well enough to recall that they had specified no such excrescence.

For a wild instant he had thought that there was a man on Jupiter already; but as he pulled up just above the platform's roof, he realized that the moving thing inside was—of course—a robot: a misshapen, many-tentacled thing about twice the size of a man. It was working busily with bottles and flasks, of which it seemed to have thousands on benches and shelves all around it. The whole enclosure was a litter of what Helmuth took to be chemical apparatus, and off to one side was an object which might have been a microscope.

The robot looked up at him and gesticulated with two or three tentacles. At first Helmuth failed to understand; then he saw that the machine was pointing to the fan-lights, and obediently turned them almost all the way down. In the resulting Jovian gloom he could see that the laboratory—for that was obviously what it was—had plenty of artificial light of its own.

There was, of course, no way that he could talk to the robot, nor it to him. If he wanted to, he could talk to the person operating it; but he knew the assignment of every man and woman on Jupiter V, and running this thing was no part of any of their duties. There was not even any provision for it on the boards——

A white light began to wink on the ghost board. That would be the incoming line for Europa. Was somebody on that snowball in charge of this many-tentacled experimenter, using Jupiter V's booster station to amplify the signals that guided it? Curiously, he plugged the jack in.

"Hello the Bridge! Who's on duty there?"

"Hello Europa. This is Bob Helmuth. Is this your robot I'm looking at, in sector ninety-four?"

"That's me," the voice said. It was impossible to avoid thinking of it as coming from the robot itself. "This is Doc Barth. How do you like my laboratory?"

"Very cosy," Helmuth said. "I didn't even know it existed. What do you do in it?"

"We just got it installed this year. It's to study the Jovian life-forms. You've seen them?"

"You mean the jellyfish? Are they really alive?"

"Yes," the robot said. "We were keeping it under our hats until we had more data, but we knew that sooner or later one of you beetle-goosers would see them. They're alive, all right. They've got a colloidal continuum-discontinuum exactly like protoplasm—except that it uses liquid ammonia as a sol substrate, instead of water."

"But what do they live on?" Helmuth said.

"Ah, that's the question. Some form of aerial plankton, that's certain; we've found the digested remnants inside them, but haven't captured any live specimens of it yet. The digested fragments don't offer us much to go on. And what does the plankton live on? I only wish I knew."

Helmuth thought about it. Life on Jupiter. It did not matter that it was simple in structure, and virtually helpless in the winds. It was life all the same, even down here in the frozen pits of a hell no living man would ever visit. And who could know, if jellyfish rode the Jovian air, what Leviathans might not swim the Jovian seas?

"You don't seem to be much impressed," the robot

said. "Jellyfish and plankton probably aren't very exciting to a layman. But the implications are tremendous. It's going to cause quite a stir among biologists, let me tell you."

"I can believe that," Helmuth said. "I was just taken aback, that's all. We've always thought of Jupiter as lifeless——"

"That's right. But now we know better. Well, back to work; I'll be talking to you." The robot flourished its tentacles and bent over a workbench.

Abstractedly, Helmuth backed the beetle off and turned it upward again. Barth, he remembered, was the man who had found a fossil on Europa. Earlier, there had been an officer doing a tour of duty in the Jovian system who had spent some of his spare time cutting soil samples, in search of bacteria. Probably he had found some; scientists of the age before spaceflight had even found them in meteors. The Earth and Mars were not the only places in the universe that would harbour life, after all; perhaps it was—everywhere. If it could exist in a place like Jupiter, there was no logical reason to rule it out even on the Sun—some animated flame no one would recognize as life. . . .

He regained the deck and sent the beetle rumbling for the switchyard; he would need to transfer to another track before he could return the car to its garage. It had occurred to him during the ghostly proxy-conversation that he had never met Doc Barth, or many of the other men with whom he had talked so often by ham radio. Except for the Bridge operators themselves, the Jovian system was a community of disembodied voices to him. And now, he would never meet them. . . .

"Wake up, Helmuth," a voice from the gang deck snapped abruptly. "If it hadn't been for me, you'd have run yourself off the end of the Bridge. You had all the automatic stops on that beetle cut out."

Helmuth reached guiltily and more than a little too late for the controls. Eva had already run his beetle back beyond the danger line.

"Sorry," he mumbled, taking the helmet off. "Thanks, Eva."

"Don't thank me. If you'd actually been in it, I'd have let it go. Less reading and more sleep is what I recommend for you, Helmuth."

"Keep your recommendations to yourself," he growled.

The incident started a new and even more disturbing chain of thought. If he were to resign now, it would be nearly a year before he could get back to Chicago. Antigravity or no antigravity, the senators' ship would have no room for unexpected extra passengers. Shipping a man back home had to be arranged far in advance. Living space had to be provided, and a cargo equivalent of the weight and space requirements he would take up on the return trip had to be dead-headed out to Jupiter V.

A year of living in the station on Jupiter V without any function—as a man whose drain on the station's supplies no longer could be justified in terms of what he did. A year of living under the eyes of Eva Chavez and Charity Dillon and the other men and women who still remained Bridge operators, men and women who would not hesitate to let him know what they thought of his quitting.

A year of living as a bystander in the feverish excitement of direct, personal exploration of Jupiter. A year of watching and hearing the inevitable deaths—while he alone stood aloof, privileged and useless. A year during which Robert Helmuth would become the most hated living entity in the Jovian system.

And, when he got back to Chicago and went looking for a job—for his resignation from the Bridge gang would automatically take him out of government service—he would be asked why he had left the Bridge at the moment when work on the Bridge was just reaching its culmination.

He began to understand why the man in the dream had volunteered.

When the trick-change bell rang, he was still determined to resign, but he had already concluded bitterly that there were, after all, other kinds of hells besides the one on Jupiter.

He was returning the board to neutral as Charity came up the cleats. Charity's eyes were snapping like a skyful of comets. Helmuth had known that they would be.

"Senator Wagoner wants to speak to you, if you're not too tired, Bob," he said. "Go ahead; I'll finish up there."

"He does?" Helmuth frowned. The dream surged back upon him. *No.* They would not rush him any faster than he wanted to go. "What about, Charity? Am I suspected of unwestern activities? I suppose you've told them how I feel."

"I have," Dillon said, unruffled. "But we've agreed that you may not feel the same way after you've talked to Wagoner. He's in the ship, of course. I've put out a suit for you at the lock."

Charity put the helmet over his head, effectively cutting himself off from further conversation, or from any further consciousness of Helmuth at all.

Helmuth stood looking at the blind, featureless

bubble on Charity's shoulders for a moment. Then, with a convulsive shrug, he went down the cleats.

Three minutes later, he was plodding in a spacesuit across the surface of Jupiter V, with the vivid bulk of the mother planet splashing his shoulders with colour.

A courteous marine let him through the ship's air-lock and deftly peeled him out of the suit. Despite a grim determination to be uninterested in the new anti-gravity and any possible consequence of it, he looked curiously about as he was conducted up toward the bow.

But the ship on the inside was like the ones that had brought him from Chicago to Jupiter V—it was like any spaceship: there was nothing in it to see but corridor walls and cleatwells, until you arrived at the cabin where you were needed.

Senator Wagoner was a surprise. He was a young man, no more than sixty at most, not at all portly, and he had the keenest pair of blue eyes that Helmuth had ever seen. The cabin in which he received Helmuth was obviously his own, a comfortable cabin as space-ship accommodations go, but neither roomy nor luxuri-ous. The senator was hard to match up with the stories Helmuth had been hearing about the current Senate, which had been involved in scandal after scandal of more than Roman proportions.

There were only two people with him: a rather plain girl who was possibly his secretary, and a tall man wearing the uniform of the Army Space Corps and the eagles of a colonel. Helmuth realized, with a second shock of surprise, that he knew the officer: he was Paige Russell, a ballistics expert who had been stationed in the Jovian system not too long ago. The dirt-collector. He smiled rather wryly as Helmuth's eyebrows went up.

Helmuth looked back at the senator. "I thought there was a whole sub-committee here," he said.

"There is, but we left them where we found them, on Ganymede. I didn't want to give you the idea that you were facing a Grand Jury," Wagoner said, smiling. "I've been forced to sit in on most of these endless loyalty investigations back home, but I can't see any point in exporting such religious ceremonies to deep space. Do sit down, Mr. Helmuth. There are drinks coming. We have a lot to talk about."

Stiffly, Helmuth sat down.

"You know Colonel Russell, of course," Wagoner said, leaning back comfortably in his own chair. "This young lady is Anne Abbott, about whom you'll hear more shortly. Now then: Dillon tells me that your usefulness to the Bridge is about at an end. In a way, I'm sorry to hear that, for you've been one of the best men we've had on any of our planetary projects. But, in another way, I'm glad. It makes you available for something much bigger, where we need you much more."

"What do you mean by that?"

"You'll have to let me explain it in my own way. First, I'd like to talk a little about the Bridge. Please don't feel that I'm quizzing you, by the way. You're at perfect liberty to say that any given question is none of my business, and I'll take no offence and hold no grudge. Also, 'I hereby disavow the authenticity of any tape or other tapping of which this statement may be a part.' In short, our conversation is unofficial, highly so."

"Thank you."

"It's to my interest; I'm hoping that you'll talk freely to me. Of course, my disavowal means nothing, since such formal statements can always be excised from a

164

tape; but later on I'm going to tell you some things you're not supposed to know, and you'll be able to judge by what I say that anything you say to me is privileged. Paige and Anne are your witnesses. Okay?"

A steward came in silently with the drinks, and left again. Helmuth tasted his. As far as he could tell, it was exactly like many he had mixed for himself back in the control shack, from standard space rations. The only difference was that it was cold, which Helmuth found startling, but not unpleasant after the first sip. He tried to relax. "I'll do my best," he said.

"Good enough. Now: Dillon says that you regard the Bridge as a monster. I've examined your dossier pretty closely—as a matter of fact I've been studying both you and Paige far more intensively than you can imagine—and I think perhaps Dillon hasn't quite the gist of your meaning. I'd like to hear it straight from you."

"I don't think the Bridge is a monster," Helmuth said slowly. "You see, Charity is on the defensive. He takes the Bridge to be conclusive evidence that no possible set of adverse conditions will ever stop man for long, and there I'm in agreement with him. But he also thinks of it as Progress, personified. He can't admit—you asked me to speak my mind, Senator—he can't admit that the West is a decadent and dying culture. All the other evidence that's available shows that it is. Charity likes to think of the Bridge as giving the lie to that evidence."

"The West hasn't many more years," Wagoner agreed, astonishingly.

Paige Russell mopped his forehead. "I still can't hear you say that," the spaceman said, "without wanting to duck under the rug. After all, MacHinery's with that pack on Ganymede——"

165

"MacHinery," Wagoner said calmly, "is probably going to die of apoplexy when we spring this thing on him, and I for one won't miss him. Anyhow, it's perfectly true; the dominoes have been falling for some time now, and the explosion Anne's outfit has cooked up is going to be the final blow. Still and all, Mr. Helmuth, the West has been responsible for some really towering achievements in its time. Perhaps the Bridge could be considered as the last and mightiest of them all."

"Not by me," Helmuth said. "The building of gigantic projects for ritual purposes—doing a thing for the sake of doing it—is the last act of an already dead culture. Look at the pyramids in Egypt for an example. Or at an even more enormous and more idiotic example, bigger than anything human beings have accomplished yet—the laying out of the 'Diagram of Power' over the whole face of Mars. If the Martians had put all that energy into survival instead, they'd probably be alive yet."

"Agreed," Wagoner said, "with reservations. 'Doing a thing for the sake of doing it' is not a definition of ritual; it's a definition of science."

"All right. That doesn't greatly alter my argument. Maybe you'll also agree that the essence of a vital culture is its ability to defend itself. The West has beaten the Soviets for half a century now—but as far as I can see, the Bridge is the West's 'Diagram of Power', its pyramids, or what have you. It shows that we're mighty, but mighty in a non-survival sort of way. All the money and the resources that went into the Bridge are going to be badly needed, *and won't be there*, when the next Soviet attack comes."

"Correction: it has already come," Wagoner said.

"And it has already won. The USSR played the greatest of all von Neumann games far better than we did, because they didn't assume as we did that each side would always choose the best strategy; they played also to wear down the players. In fifty years of unrelenting pressure, they succeeded in converting the West into a system so like the Soviets' as to make direct military action unnecessary; we Sovietized ourselves, and our moves are now exactly predictable.

"So in part I agree with you. What we needed was to sink the energy and the money into the game—into social research, since the menace was social. Instead, typically, we put it into a physical research project of unprecedented size. Which was, of course, just what the theory of games said we would do. For a man who's been cut off from Earth for years, Helmuth, you seem to know more about what's going on down there than most of the general populace does."

"Nothing promotes an interest in Earth like being off it," Helmuth said. "And there's plenty of time to read out here." Either the drink was stronger than he had expected—which was reasonable, considering that he had been off the stuff for some time now—or the senator's calm concurrence in the collapse of Helmuth's entire world had given him another shove toward the abyss; his head was spinning.

Wagoner saw it. He leaned forward suddenly, catching Helmuth flat-footed. *"However,"* he said, "it's difficult for me to agree that the Bridge serves, or ever did serve, a ritual purpose. The Bridge served several huge practical purposes which are now fulfilled. As a matter of fact, the Bridge, as such, is now a defunct project."

"Defunct?" Helmuth said faintly.

"Quite. Of course, we'll continue to operate it for a

while. You can't stop a process of that size on a dime. Besides, one of the reasons why we built the Bridge was because the USSR expected us to; the game said that we should launch another Manhattan District or H-bomb project at this point, and we hated to disappoint them. One thing we are *not* going to do this time, however, is to tell them the problem that the project was supposed to solve—let alone that it *can* be solved, and has been.

"So we'll keep the Bridge going, physically and publically. That'll be just as well, too, for people like Dillon who are emotionally tied up in it, above and beyond their conditioning to it. You're the only person in authority in the whole station who's already lost enough interest in the Bridge to make it safe for me to tell you that it's being abandoned."

"But why?"

"Because," Wagoner went on quietly, "the Bridge has now given us confirmation of a theory of stupendous importance—so important, in my opinion, that the imminent fall of the West seems like a puny event in comparison. A confirmation, incidentally, which contains in it the seeds of ultimate destruction for the Soviets, whatever they may win for themselves in the next hundred years or so."

"I suppose," Helmuth said, puzzled, "that you mean antigravity?"

For the first time, it was Wagoner's turn to be taken aback. "Man," he said at last, "do you know *everything* I want to tell you? I hope not, or my conclusions will be mighty unwelcome to both of us. Do you also know what an anti-agathic is?"

"No," Helmuth said. "I don't even recognize the root of the word."

"Well, that's a relief. But surely Charity didn't tell you we had antigravity. I strictly enjoined him not to mention it."

"No. The subject's been on my mind," Helmuth said. "But I certainly don't see why it should be so world-shaking, any more than I see how the Bridge helped to bring it about. I thought it would be developed independently, for the further exploitation of the Bridge. In other words, to put men down there, and short-circuit this remote control operation we have on Jupiter V. And I thought it would step up Bridge operation, not discontinue it."

"Not at all. Nobody in his right mind would want to put men on Jupiter, and besides, gravity isn't the main problem down there. Even eight gravities is perfectly tolerable for short periods of time—and anyhow a man in a pressure suit couldn't get five hundred miles down through that atmosphere before he'd be as buoyed up and weightless as a fish—and even more thoroughly at the mercy of the currents."

"And you can't screen out the pressure?"

"We can," Wagoner said, "but only at ruinous cost. Besides, there'd be no point in trying. The Bridge is finished. It's given us information in thousands of different categories, much of it very valuable indeed. But the one job that *only* the Bridge could do was that of confirming, or throwing out, the Blackett-Dirac equations."

"Which are——?"

"They show a relationship between magnetism and the spinning of a massive body—that much is the Dirac part of it. The Blackett Equation seemed to show that the same formula also applied to gravity; it says G equals $(2CP/BU)^2$, where C is the velocity of light, P is magnetic moment, and U is angular momentum. B is an uncertainty correction, a constant which amounts to 0·25.

"If the figures we collected on the magnetic field strength of Jupiter forced us to retire the equations, then none of the rest of the information we've gotten from the Bridge would have been worth the money we spent to get it. On the other hand, Jupiter was the only body in the solar system available to us which was big enough in all relevant respects to make it possible for us to test those equations at all. They involve quantities of infinitesimal orders of magnitudes.

"And the figures showed that Dirac was right. *They also show that Blackett was right.* Both magnetism *and* gravity are phenomena of rotation.

"I won't bother to trace the succeeding steps, because I think you can work them out for yourself. It's enough to say that there's a drive-generator on board this ship which is the complete and final justification of all the hell you people on the Bridge have been put through. The gadget has a long technical name, but the technies who tend it have already nicknamed it the spindizzy, because of what it does to the magnetic moment of any atom—*any* atom—within its field.

"While it's in operation, it absolutely refuses to notice any atom outside its own influence. Furthermore, it will notice no other strain or influence which holds good beyond the borders of that field. It's so snooty that it has to be stopped down to almost nothing when it's brought close to a planet, or it won't let you land. But in deep space . . . well, it's impervious to meteors and such trash, of course; it's impervious to gravity; and—it hasn't the faintest interest in any legislation about top speed limits. It moves in its own continuum, not in the general frame."

"You're kidding," Helmuth said.

"Am I, now? This ship came to Ganymede directly from Earth. It did it in a little under two hours, counting manœuvring time. That means that most of the way we made about 55,000 miles per second—with the spindizzy drawing less than five watts of power out of three ordinary No. 6 dry cells."

Helmuth took a defiant pull at his drink. "This thing really has no top speed at all?" he said. "How can you be sure of that?"

"Well, we can't," Wagoner admitted. "After all, one of the unfortunate things about general mathematical formulae is that they don't contain cut-off points to warn you of areas where they don't apply. Even quantum mechanics is somewhat subject to that criticism. However, we expect to know pretty soon just how fast the spindizzy can drive an object. We expect you to tell us."

"I?"

"Yes, you, and Colonel Russell, and Miss Abbott too, I hope." Helmuth looked at the other two; both of them looked at least as stunned as he felt. He could not imagine why. "The coming débâcle on Earth makes it absolutely imperative for us—the West—to get interstellar expeditions started at once. Richardson Observatory, on the Moon, has two likely-looking systems mapped already—one at Wolf 359, the other at 61 Cygni—and there are sure to be others, hundreds of others, where Earth-like planets are highly probable.

"What we're doing, in a nutshell, is evacuating the West—not physically, of course, but in essence, in idea. We want to scatter adventurous people, people with a thoroughly indoctrinated love of being free, all over this part of the galaxy, if it can be done.

"Once they're out there, they'll be free to flourish,

171

with no interference from Earth. The Soviets haven't the spindizzy yet, and even after they get it, they won't dare allow it to be used. It's too good and too final an escape route for disaffected comrades.

"What we want you to do, Helmuth . . . now I'm getting to the point, you see . : . is to direct this exodus, with Colonel Russell's help. You've the intelligence and the cast of mind for it. Your analysis of the situation on Earth confirms that, if any more confirmation were needed. And—there's no future for you on Earth now."

"You'll have to excuse me for a while," Helmuth said firmly. "I'm in no condition to be reasonable now; it's been more than I could digest in a few moments. And the decision doesn't entirely rest with me, either. If I could give you an answer in . . . let me see . . . about three hours. Will that be soon enough?"

"That'll be fine," the senator said.

For a moment after the door closed behind Helmuth there was silence in the senator's cabin. At last Paige said:

"So it was long life for spacemen you were after, all the time. Long life, by God, for *me*, and for the likes of me."

Wagoner nodded. "This was the one part of this affair that I couldn't explain to you back in Tru Gunn's office," he said. "Until you had ridden in this ship, and understood as a spaceman just what kind of a thing we have in it, you wouldn't have believed me; Helmuth does, you see, because he already has the background. In the same way, I didn't go into the question of the anti-agathic with Helmuth, because that's something he's going to have to experience; you two have the background to understand that part of it through explanation alone.

"Now you see why I didn't give a whistle about your spy, Paige. The Soviets can have the Earth. As a matter of fact they will take it before very long, whether we give it to them or not. But we are going to scatter the West throughout the stars, scatter it with immortal people carrying immortal ideas. People like you, and Miss Abbott."

Paige looked back to Anne. She was aloofly regarding the empty space just above Wagoner's head, as though still looking at the bewhiskered picture of the Pfitzner founder which hung in Gunn's office. There was something in her face, however, that Paige could read. He smothered a grin and said: "Why me?"

"Because you're just what we need for the job. I don't mind telling you that your blundering into the Pfitzner project in the first place was an act of Providence from my point of view. When Anne first called your qualifications to my attention, I was almost prepared to believe that they'd been faked. You're going to be liaison-man between the Pfitzner side of the project and the Bridge side. We've got the total output to date of both ascomycin and the new anti-agathic salted away in the cargo-hold, and Anne's already shown you how to take the stuff and how to administer it to others. After that—just as soon as you and Helmuth can work out the details—the stars are yours."

"Anne," Paige said. She turned her head slowly toward him. "Are you with this thing?"

"I'm here," she said. "And I'd had a few inklings of what was up before. You were the one who had to be brought in, not I."

Paige thought about it a moment more. Then something both very new and very old occurred to him.

"Senator," he said, "you've gone to an immense

amount of trouble to make this whole thing possible—but I don't think you plan to go with us."

"No, Paige, I don't. For one thing, MacHinery and his crew will regard the whole project as treasonous. If it's to be carried out nevertheless, someone has to stay behind and be the goat—and after all, the idea *was* mine, so I'm the logical candidate." He felt silent for a moment. Then he added, ruminatively: "The government boys have nobody but themselves to thank for this. The whole project would never have been possible as long as the West had a government of laws and not of men, and stuck to it. It was a long while ago that some people—MacHinery's grandfather among them—set themselves up to be their own judges of whether or not a law ought to be obeyed. They had precedents. And now here we are, on the brink of the most enormous breach of our social contract the West has ever had to suffer—and the West can't stop it." He smiled suddenly. "I'll have good use for that argument in the court."

Anne was on her feet, her eyes suddenly wet, her lower lip just barely trembling. Evidently, over whatever time she had known Wagoner and had known what he had planned, it had never occurred to her that the young-old senator might stay behind.

"That's no good!" she said in a low voice. "They won't listen, and you know it. They might easily hang you for it. If they find you guilty of treason, they'll seal you up in the pile-waste dump—that's the current penalty, isn't it? You can't go back!"

"It's a phony terror. Pile wastes are quick chemical poisons; you don't last long enough to notice that they're also hot," Wagoner said. "And what difference does it make, anyhow? Nothing and nobody can harm me now. The job is done."

Anne put her hands to her face.

"Besides, Anne," Wagoner said, with gentle insistence, "the stars are for young people—eternally young people. An eternal oldster would be an anachronism."

"Why—did you do it, then?" Paige said. His own voice was none too steady.

"Why?" Wagoner said. "You know the answer to that, Paige. You've known it all your life. I could see it in your face, as soon as I told Helmuth that we were going out to the stars. Supposing you tell *me* what it is."

Anne swung her blurred eyes on Paige. He thought he knew what she expected to hear him say; they had talked about it often enough, and it was what he once would have said himself. But now another force seemed to him to be the stronger: a special thing, bearing the name of no established dogma, but nevertheless and unmistakably the force to which he had borne allegiance all his life. He in his turn could see it in Wagoner's face now, and he knew he had seen it before in Anne's.

"It's the thing that lures monkeys into cages," he said slowly. "And lures cats into open desk drawers and up telephone poles. It's driven men to conquer death, and put the stars into our hands. I suppose that I'd call it Curiosity."

Wagoner looked startled. "Is that really what you want to call it?" he said. "Somehow it seems insufficient; I should have given it another name. Perhaps you'll amend it later, somewhere, some day out by Aldebaran."

He stood up and looked at the two for a moment in silence. Then he smiled.

"And now," he said gently, "*nunc dimittis . . .* suffer thy servant to depart in peace."

"And so, that's the story," Helmuth said.

Eva remained silent in her chair for a long time.

"One thing I don't understand," she said at last. "Why did you come to me? I'd have thought that you'd find the whole thing terrifying."

"Oh, it's terrifying, all right," Helmuth said, with quiet exultation. "But terror and fright are two different things, as I've just discovered. We were both wrong, Evita. I was wrong in thinking that the Bridge was a dead end. You were wrong in thinking of it as an end in itself."

"I don't understand you."

"I didn't understand myself. My fears of working in person on the Bridge were irrational; they came from dreams. That should have tipped me off right away. There was really never any chance of anyone's working in person on Jupiter; but *I wanted to*. It was a death-wish, and it came directly out of the goddamned conditioning. I knew, we all knew, that the Bridge couldn't stand for ever, but we were conditioned to believe that it had to. Nothing else could justify the awful ordeal of keeping it going even one day. The result: the classical dilemma that leads to madness. It affected you, too, and your response was just as insane as mine: you wanted to have a child here.

"Now all that's changed. The work the Bridge was doing was worth while after all. I was wrong in calling it a bridge to nowhere. And Eva, you no more saw where it was going than I did, or you'd never have made it the be-all and end-all of your existence.

"Now, there's a place to go to. In fact, there are places—hundreds of places. They'll be Earthlike places. Since the Soviets are about to win the Earth, those places will be more Earthlike than Earth itself, at least for the next century or so!"

She said: "Why are you telling me this? Just to make peace between us?"

"I'm going to take on this job, Evita . . . if you'll go along."

She turned swiftly, rising out of the chair with a marvellous fluidity of motion. At the same instant, all the alarm bells in the station went off at once, filling every metal cranny with a jangle·of pure horror.

"*Posts!*" the loudspeaker above Eva's bed roared, in a distorted, gigantic caricature of Charity Dillon's voice. "*Peak storm overload! The STD is now passing the Spot. Wild velocity has already topped all previous records, and part of the land mass has begun to settle. This is an A-1 overload emergency.*"

Behind Charity's bellow, they could hear what he was hearing, the winds of Jupiter, a spectrum of continuous, insane shrieking. The Bridge was responding with monstrous groans of agony. There was another sound, too, an almost musical cacophony of sharp, percussive tones, such as a dinosaur might make pushing its way through a forest of huge steel tuning-forks. Helmuth had never heard the sound before, but he knew what it was.

The deck of the Bridge was splitting up the middle.

177

After a moment more, the uproar dimmed, and the speaker said, in Charity's normal voice: "Eva, you too, please. Acknowledge, please. This is it—unless everybody comes on duty at once, the Bridge may go down within the next hour."

"Let it," Eva responded quietly.

There was a brief, startled silence, and then a ghost of a human sound. The voice was Senator Wagoner's, and the sound just might have been a chuckle.

Charity's circuit clicked out.

The mighty death of the Bridge continued to resound in the little room.

After a while, the man and the woman went to the window, and looked past the discarded bulk of Jupiter at the near horizon, where there had always been visible a few stars.

CODA

CODA

"Every end", Wagoner wrote on the wall of his cell on the last day, "is a new beginning. Perhaps in a thousand years my Earthmen will come home again. Or in two thousand, or four, if they still remember home then. They'll come back, yes; but I hope they won't stay. I pray they will not stay."

He looked at what he had written and thought of signing his name. While he debated that, he made the mark for the last day on his calendar, and the point on his stub of pencil struck stone under the calcimine and snapped, leaving nothing behind it but a little coronet of frayed, dirty blond wood. He could wear that away against the window-ledge, at least enough to expose a little graphite, but instead he dropped the stub in the waste can.

There was writing enough in the stars that he could see, because he had written it there. There was a constellation called Wagoner, and every star in the sky belonged to it. That was surely enough.

Later that day, a man named MacHinery said: "Bliss Wagoner is dead."

As usual, MacHinery was wrong.